I0623630

# A TIME TO SHINE

By
## Donovan D. Corzo
Corzo Creations, LLC

Dedicated to the love of my life, Kam.

Many thanks to the Tuesday night crowd for letting me bend your ears.

To Shari, who gave me that pen and told me to go and write that novel. I did, and here it is.

To the staff of "The Book Rack," thanks for letting me hang out for inspiration and research.

To all my family and friends. Thanks for believing in me and for reading the many rough drafts.

To Karl, my friend for over 30 years and my unofficial editor. I appreciate your honesty and experience.

To my Editor, Lila Waterfield, "Thanks for making it POP!"

To the Cover Designer Adeel Ahmad, "Thanks for making them Shine."

# Other Titles by the Author

**Traveller Role-Playing Game Supplements:**
100 Plots E-Book: 978-1-958297-04-9, Paperback: 978-1-958297-05-6
100 Rendezvous E-Book: 978-1-958297-07-0,
Paperback: 978-1-958297-08-7
100 Alien Rendezvous (forthcoming)
100 Alien Plots (in the works)
100 Underworld Rendezvous **eBook ISBN: 978-1-958297-10-0**

# Patrol Craft Series

**Shine On: Invasion USA:** E-Book ISBN: 978-1-958297-06-3
Paperback: ISBN: 978-1-958297-12-4
Hardcover: ISBN: 978-1-958297-09-4
Audiobook: ISBN: 978-1-958297-13-1
**Shining Through: Battles in the Pacific**
E-Book: ISBN: 978-1-958297-25-4
Paperback: ISBN: 978-1-958297-26-1
Hardcover: ISBN: 978-1-958297-27-8
Audiobook: ISBN: 978-1-958297-51-3
**Up in the Clouds**: E-Book: ISBN: 978-1-958297-54-4
Paperback: ISBN: 978-1-958297-55-1
Hardcover: ISBN: 978-1-958297
Audiobook: ISBN: 978-1-958297

# Forthcoming Novels

**Peace Reigns Through**
**The Wars End**

# Contents

# A Time to Shine

This novel is a work of fiction. All resemblances to persons, living or dead, are incidental; any interactions with historical events & or persons are entirely fictional. All dialogue comes from my imagination. This work was copyrighted in 2021 by Donovan D. Corzo.

All rights reserved, including the right to reproduce this book in any form or portion thereof.

ISBN Hardback: 978-1-958297-02-5
ISBN Paperback: 978-1-958297-01-8
ISBN E-Book: 978-1-958297-00-1
ISBN Audiobook: 978-1-958297-03-2
Registered Trademark through Corzo Creations, LLC

# Foreword

I have done ample research and have provided a bibliography of sources. I have attempted to follow history closely and stay true to form, but my days may be slightly off. I have tried to follow the military protocols and expectations. However, I have taken liberties with some subject matter because if I didn't, the protagonists would still be in college or training until the war is over.

The main reason I wrote this novel is that when I read fiction, they always talk about the heroes going off to Gunnery School or Command School, taking a Course in Combat and Tactics, but have yet to go into detail about what that is like. Therefore, I wrote one and made them more believable. Heroes aren't always out saving the world. They must buy groceries and deal with everyday life, too. I hope you enjoy reading this and subsequent novels in the series or set in the same period.

**Note:** This novel uses period dialogue, including racial slurs. They are spoken between persons, in films, on the radio, and written in mass media. If the truth of history offends you, don't read any further.

# USS ABERDEEN: Morning Watch Underway Heading to the Coral Sea

Daniel Core stared at the coffee cup dregs and felt the turbines speed up. He was dressed in a Navy work uniform, a soft collar chambray shirt with bell-bottom dungaree material pants, a navy blue knit belt, and a cover also dyed Navy blue to protect it from heavy soiling generally only worn by the gunnery and engine room departments. He focused on the Vmail that his mother had sent him. A new way of corresponding with soldiers, seamen, and airmen stationed abroad used a standardized stationery template incorporating the letter and envelope together. They were filled out, copied to film, sent to the destination, enlarged, and printed. This reduced the cost and space for mail; thousands of letters could be combined into a few rolls of film.

| | |
|---|---|
| VM    To: Daniel Core | From Penelope Core |
| Destroyer USS Aberdeen | 1315 Ashley Phosphate Rd. |
| Pacific Fleet, Pearl Harbor | Charleston, SC |

December 17, 1941

Dearest Son,
I have not heard from you and worry you need to eat more. We learned of Pearl Harbor's devastation and hope you are well. There is so much talk about an invasion, and rumors are flying. Your brothers have joined the Marines and Army, respectively. Midora has also decided to serve and has joined the WAVES. So many of my children have joined the war effort, and I can say nothing. I know that you are doing what you must to protect us all. I am proud of you all. With much love,
Mother

'There's that wicked shimmy again,' he thought as he felt the ship's deck plates shift. "They need to get that handled." He pocketed the letter, grabbed his metal tray, and placed it and the heavy porcelain coffee cup missing a handle in their respective places. He headed for the turret at frame 5, Gun 1.

It was an older ship commissioned in the 1930s when the treaties declared she could only be so many tons. But she was built with two oiler stacks instead of the typical four. She used updated steam injection technologies to increase turbine rotation plus a 22% increase from the earlier classes. There were only eight officers and a full battle complement of 250 other ranks, 50 Marines. They were performing escort duties to and from Australia.

He remembered last week when they had been moored alongside the USS Minneapolis during the attack at Pearl Harbor, dispatched several aircraft, and helped sink a mini-submarine in the bay. Then, they charged forward to set up a screen to protect the bay against a third wave that never came.

"That was a hell of a day," he thought as he made the usual twists and turned to get to his duty station across the 377-foot-long and forty feet wide ship.

He had joined the Navy in 1939 when he witnessed German U-boats sinking ships from a convoy launched from Charleston, SC, headed to Britain. He even had a Captain's ticket as his grandfather had been a tugboat captain and wanted to leave the business to a family member, and he had been the only one interested. So, he had worked tirelessly to earn that Captain's Certificate, and then the world went crazy. After witnessing the destruction of the ships, he went home, and when he walked in, his grandfather just knew. He didn't have to say anything. He just got up and began packing a seabag, handing it to him.

"If a good man does nothing, then that is evil enough. Go forth and help conquer that evil. But remember, you will only be a wheel in a cog. They will tell you your place. Please don't fight with them or argue because cream rises, no matter what. Your time will come." They got in the truck and headed to the induction site. He disembarked, never looking back. The Navy sent him to basic, then on to gunnery school. He made it to the rate of second class and was rather good at what he did but always struggled with math. He had an eidetic memory, so he could call up tables if he had read them at least once, which significantly helped him in life. The Navy was not interested in his Captain's ticket because he had yet to go to college, nor did he even know any of the right people, so being an officer was right out. They wouldn't even consider him for a Warrant Officer, which he felt was a little unfair, but then he remembered his grandfather's wisdom and just shrugged it off.

"Hey, Core?" called a voice from behind a cabinet.

"Yeah, Cortez?"

"Here's your fiver from last night's game," a smallish Mexican American from Los Angeles said as he slapped the currency into his hand. He was dark and swarthy compared to Daniel's ghost-white complexion. His black hair - not quite curly or straight - wouldn't commit, but the Navy haircut took care of that.

"How did you know?" Cortez asked.

"Know what?" asked Daniel.

"That they were going to win?" said Cortez.

"It just seemed like it was their time. After all, the cream rises!"

"Ejo de puta.," Cortez said half-jokingly. (*You son of a bitch.*)

"Yo, intiendes tu dece," (*I understood what you said*) Daniel said with a half-smile as he sat at the desk and pulled out the file on the ammunition expenditures. Switching to English, he said, "We've been firing our guns almost too much lately, and if we don't watch it, the bores will crack, and it will be back to the yards to replace them."

"So what? Then we leave this 'Mierda' and get a few weeks of Liberty in San Diego. We can get some good tamales and Chorizo plus Horchata, which we could use in this heat."

"You got that right. Horchata would be nice. But sometimes it's too much, too sweet and filling. I prefer just a plain coconut cooled under ice, top sliced off with a straw in it," he said as he undid his top button and pointed the desk fan towards himself.

The overhead Klaxon went off. "GENERAL QUARTERS! GENERAL QUARTERS! Aircraft spotted! All hands to Battle Stations!"

They both jumped up and scrambled to reach Turret 1, right outside their office, donning helmets and life vests. They jumped inside and battened down the hatch. They climbed into their seats, donning communications gear. As soon as the hatch was dogged, the light switched to the red bulb, indicating battle mode. Their job was to coordinate the ship's fire control to the target. They had an Officer above them, but he oversaw four-127 mm guns. His name was Mr. Begley, and his voice came over the comm. "Turret 1- target bearing 472- Azmuth 151.3. Mark!"

"Turret 1-target 151.3 Aye!" they called out in unison.

"What say you?" he asked.

Looking through the scope, Daniel saw the outline of what appeared to be a minesweeper or oiler from the Japanese Navy. "Sokaitai!" he called.

"FIRE!" came the order.

"FIRING!" he yelled as his foot stomped on the mechanism, and a 127mm shell was launched toward the enemy. Clicking and whirring noises sounded as the ammunition elevator raised a shell and a powder bag, and two crewmen lifted them out and placed them into the firing chute.

He could hear the Antiaircraft guns firing outside. But he had to focus on the task at hand. "Firing, firing," he called out as he mashed the pedal twice. Then, they waited.

"Miss! Close! Hit! Keep firing. We got the range right!"

So, they did. They kept it up until the command, "Turret One-Cease Firing! She's done for." He heard and felt the explosion across the water slam into his turret. "Turret One-here. How close were we, sir?"

"They crossed the T!" Mr. Begley called out, meaning they had lined up perfectly for destruction.

He was glad but sad as they had just killed or doomed 200-300 people, but he reminded himself that was the price of war. "If they hadn't attacked us, we wouldn't be in this mess!" A dark look crossed his face as they stowed the gear and returned to the office. Mr. Begley was already there, looking incredibly pleased with himself. He was a good officer who kept track of his men: a typical tall, lean blond from a Navy family, Annapolis graduate, Captain of the Football team, and wearing the khaki uniform of the day. As he whipped out his notebook, Cortez reflexively jumped to the typewriter and loaded it with paper. As soon as it was charged, Mr. Begley said, "Morning watch after-action report. 07:38 General Quarters sounded. Aircraft spotted approaching DU-Greg 151. Turrets 1 through 4 responded to sightings of several Maru to the lee. They were targeted and destroyed as they Crossed the T. 31 rounds were expended, and 5 minutes elapsed until contact was broken. AA gun emplacements under command downed five enemy fighters. Approximately 450 rounds were expended. No torpedoes were launched as an approach not attainable. Convoy suffered no losses. "

"Send it!" he stated, holding his hand for the copy and leaving the compartment to deliver it to the Captain. Daniel retrieved his copy, running down the corridor to the radio shack that would encrypt it and send it back to Pearl.

# Midwatch

Daniel and Cortez were just in the middle of the mess hall when Mr. Begley walked up to them, motioning for them to follow him. They complied, and he took them to the front of the chow line and signaled the cook. He came forward with two trays full of steak and potatoes. They both looked at the perfectly prepared steaks, and their mouths watered.

Mr. Begley whistled loudly and said, "Now hear this! Turret 1 sank a minesweeper this morning, and they are rewarded with steak. Do your job right, and you will eat well, too. That is all." He motioned for them to sit at an unoccupied table. The crew members looked on as they ate chipped beef on wheat toast. Also known as SOS – 'Shit on a Shingle.' But no one was jealous. They were glad for their brethren. But they also knew the steaks would be tough. So, they smiled and nodded at the good fortune, knowing their turn would come.

Two others joined them at the table- Chris McConnell, a tall, skinny man from Pennsylvania who was of Armenian stock, and Steve McCaskill, a ghost white man of 5'4" with curly black hair and just a dusting of freckles across his face- who were the loaders for the 5-inch guns. Chris smiled at the steak. Daniel nodded, cut it in half, and forked it over. Chris nodded at Cortez, who leaned over his plate and said, "No way, man. It's been too long." He looked longingly at the steak.

"That's not quite fair. They loaded the shells that we fired," said Daniel

"Too bad! Plus, I had my wisdom teeth removed last time we won steaks, so it's even!" replied Cortez.

Chris nodded, then cut his steak in half and gave it to Steve.

"Queen to Bishop six, check," said Daniel.

"Knight takes Queen," replied Chris.

Steve had pulled out a small travel chessboard and used a book to hide it. They had to rely on their memories for this game. Steve looked over the board, recording the moves and checking for accuracy.

"Bishop to King 7, check," said Daniel.

Most of the lunch-goers were now crowding around and beginning to place bets.

"Bishop to King 7, checkmate!" called Daniel triumphantly.

Chris needed clarification. He said to Steve," Verify!"

"Verified!" replied Steve dejectedly.

Chris reached over to shake Daniels's hand when an explosion rocked the ship—lifting it and slamming it down. Red emergency lights popped on, and they scrambled to their feet as the secondaries went off. The boat rocked and leaned hard to starboard. Screaming could be heard over the con. "Get replacements to the bridge; Daniel Core, report to the bridge!"

He rushed forth past the confusion and tried to block out the destruction. When he arrived, the bridge was no more. It had been peeled back, and the wind was whipping about; a shocked helmsman named Restivo was frozen in place. "What are your orders?" He called out.

Mr. Begley was lying in the Captain's Battle Cabin bed with blood pouring from his chest. His face was wan and tight. He motioned for Daniel to come forth. "We got hammered! All the officers are dead. I'm promoting you to Warrant with acting Captaincy. Choose the replacements from what is left of the crew and fight the ship!" His voice rasped, and blood filled his mouth.

"Sir?"

"The Captain himself wrote the orders. You were our backup plan. Here's the battlefield commission. He wrote it when you struck for Warrant. Don't mess it up," he said as he pressed a manila envelope into Daniel's hands. He reached up and pinned the rank to his collar.

"Helm, I stand relieved," he called out as he died.

"Helm, what's our heading?" Daniel asked crisply, trying to stay focused.

"192," he yelled back.

Daniel reached over to the com and hit the switch. "Now hear this! Damage reports to the bridge by runner. All officers are dead. I, Daniel Core, am now in charge and acting Captain. I need all trained reserve personnel to the bridge. Repair parties and fire control teams report to your stations. All Marines split into parties of 10 and help in any way possible." He closed the switch.

"Helm, what hit us?"

"Two torpedoes and a big bomb." The helmsman winced as a corpsman applied a large bandage to his cheek.

Daniel could hear the replacement crew members pulling bodies out of the way and dragging them down the corridor. Buckets of sand were tossed liberally around. They could wash the blood and entrails later. Right now, they just needed to survive.

The next few minutes flew by as he ascertained the damage to the ship and attempted to keep pace with the convoy and keep the lookouts busy, watching for everything. He knew that they had to reduce speed to help fight the fire. If he went too fast, it would just fan the flames. "Helm reduce speed by 50 percent."

"Reducing speed by 50 percent, aye."

"Helm, What's our speed now?"

"Uhm, 20 knots, sir."

"Good! Keep her there."

He heard the sound of a freight train crashing directly in their path and saw the lead cruiser take a hit from a shell that exploded into a gun mount. The cruiser was rent open, white steam escaping from jagged holes as he saw her list to one side.

He called the order out, "Helm hard starboard. Avoid hitting that cruiser and screen her from further attack!"

"Hard to starboard, Aye!" the helmsman called out expertly.

"JESUS CHRIST! Collision, COLLISION! Ship to Port" called a watcher.

"HELM HARD, LEEWARD!" Daniel screamed as a destroyer loomed from the white fog spilling out of the cruiser. They barely missed each other as collision alarms and bells rang out.

Suddenly, they heard a "WHUMP" sound as a small support ship slammed into something and exploded. The radio said, "CONVOY, CONVOY; you're in a minefield! All craft head east now! EXECUTE!" He saw a PBY buzz by and was grateful for the assistance. Those Amphibious planes resembled albatrosses and were their eyes in the deep.

He gave the order, and the ship veered wildly to the side, and he heard her groan. He also saw HMS 136 and HMS 119 laying down a smokescreen to help protect the cruiser. DD134 drifted through the fog, and he heard a rattle and whump, then saw the ship lift and slam down again. He called to the lookout, "What just happened to 134?"

"They rolled a depth charge overboard, and it exploded too close underneath her and took out her propellers."

"All 5-inch guns fire to protect 134!" he called out.

"Why aren't they finishing us off?" he called to no one. Then he walked over to the port side and saw roiling smoke from multiple rends in the ship. He realized this was now the fog of war, and they couldn't hit what they couldn't see.

"Helm, come to 162, head for the atoll anchorage. "

"Maru sighted on the starboard side," called a replacement crewman. The Maru, a converted Merchant ship, sported guns and torpedoes.

"Marines report to rear starboard side armed to repel all boarding parties," he called out. The order was relayed through the PA system.

"All antiaircraft guns open up on that, Maru! Fire for effect!" he said. He heard a different type of boom starting to ring out from the ship's rear. "Waisner, what's that booming?" he asked.

"It's the Marines, sir. They are using anti-tank weapons," Waisner, a beefy Scotsman from Salkehatchie, SC, replied.

"Well, that's creative," he said.

"Sir, Commodore requests an update!" called out the radio operator.

Daniel walked over to the phone and picked it up. "Sir?"

"Why are you out of position?" asked the Commodore.

"Sir, we are this side of mortally wounded. All officers are dead. I'm the acting Captain and heading for the atoll for emergency repairs, but we are beating off a Maru."

"Who are you?" the Commodore asked.

"Daniel Core, Gunners Mate First Class."

"All officers?" asked the Commodore

"Yes, sir!" he replied

"Why you?" the Commodore asked.

"I have a commercial Captain's ticket. I've got to go!" He left the line open and tended to the fight.

"Helm come about to 156. Fire torpedoes as she bears." The ship had two torpedo launchers stacked three on each side amidships. The destroyer had to veer off to one sch electrically to fire.

He saw the Maru getting raked with gunfire; it listed to the side as torpedoes slammed into her until it blew into pieces.

He heard the crew cheer as they saw the wreckage. But he knew they were not out of the woods yet. They still had to contend with the fires aboard the ship. He gave the order for the announcement. "All hands clear from action stations and report to the fire brigade." They were still making the best speed for the atoll, and he called to the Yeoman manning the chart, "How long till we reach the Atoll?"

"At this speed, about two hours, sir."

"Good. Carry on."

When the fires were put out, he started to relax a bit. Another hour later, they were in the clear. He saw two fighter aircraft in a combat air patrol. Now, he had accomplished his mission. He had fought the ship, the fires, the sea, and the enemy and got his crew to safety.

"Ease the rudder to 10", he called

"Easing to 10.", replied the helmsman.

"All hands to quarters. Bring ship to anchor," he called out, and the orders were relayed to the division.

He saw the atoll and parked the ship. The USS Minnetonka pulled up to screen him, and they launched a gig.

"Side boys report amidships to receive the party," he ordered, and it was piped through.

"I need a list of all remaining crew," he looked at the replacements and called out. "Coxswain Sherman, you have the bridge."

"Aye, sir," he replied as he gulped.

Daniel left the bridge and received the guest; a yeoman in a crisp white uniform was piped aboard when he arrived. He handed a file to Daniel as he said, "With the Commodore's compliments. You are to report to Pearl for debriefing. Bring a list of casualties, witnesses, and all replacement personnel brevetted up in rank. You have two hours."

"Acknowledged; I need to sound the ship," he stated.

"Noted. We will wait." said the Yeoman.

He turned and went to meet the carpenter. Carpenter was meaningless on a modern warship since they were made from steel plates riveted and welded in place. It was a carryover from when they were made of wood. He was a structural engineer. But the name stuck.

With the reports in hand, Daniel grabbed helmsman Restivo and disembarked. The gig was a small motorboat that was comfortable and could seat twelve. The canvas was up due to the sun; he felt the breeze and the humidity. But he couldn't enjoy the ride. Too much had happened in too little time, and it would upend his world forever. Twenty minutes later, they were shuttled aboard the Commodores ship. He met them and took the packet.

Beaming with pride, he clapped Daniel on the shoulder. "You did well out, their son! You stepped up, fought off the bastards, and got the ship to the atoll," he said as they turned and headed for the main briefing room, which was appointed with wood panels everywhere. Once there, they were all seated around the table. Lucky Strikes Cigarettes were pulled out, and he was offered one but refused.

"Just for the record, tell me what happened," the Commodore said.

So, Daniel told the tale, leaving nothing out. "We had engaged the enemy at 07:32, downed two planes, and sunk a "Sokaitai." I was in the mess hall aft of turret one when the ship was hit. I was ordered to the bridge where Mr. Begley promoted me to Warrant with acting Captaincy to get the crew to safety and fight the ship."

Commodore King looked to Restivo when he was finished and asked, "Is that true?" The cigarette smoke was up near the lights and left a hazy fog.

Restivo nodded.

"Say it out loud, please, for the record," asked the Commodore.

Restivo turned red and replied, "Yes, sir, every word."

"Good. I'm satisfied. Now, Yeoman Randsom will take you to quarters to get cleaned up. You will have new uniforms," he said, then gestured to Restivo's cheek. "And get that seen to. Within the next four hours, you will leave for Pearl with the mail run."

They stood, saluted, and departed. Restivo was spun off to medical, and Daniel was sent to the officers' quarters. A full Dopp kit, a complete navy Grey Warrant Officers' uniform, skivvies, undershirt, and assorted sundries were laid out on the bed when he arrived. He grabbed what he needed and then headed for the shower. Fully dressed, he went in search of chow. Since it was between meals, only coffee and bologna sandwiches were available.

He grabbed a cup and a couple of sandwiches and sat down. He was alive and alone with his thoughts for the first time in 12 hours. He ate without tasting the food and drank the coffee. It was in very delicate chintz cups, unlike the thick ceramic he had been used to. There were even sugar cubes and fresh cream available. He noticed cold drinks on ice and an honor box for the nickels. He dug one out and grabbed a 12 oz. Hires Root Beer. It tasted good and had a sharp tang.

A couple of officers drifted in, and he rose. They quickly sized him up and nodded. "You're the brevet Captain?" asked the taller one.

"Yes, sir," he replied.

"We're all officers here. Just the last name will be fine. Anyway, come see the tailor to get you squared away."

"I thought I could take care of that in Pearl," he said.

"Nope, you will go directly to Admiral Nimitz's Office. No delay. Harold will get your measurements and officers' kit drawn from stores; your sizes will be listed on each garment so they can be sent directly to the tailors in Pearl when you land. You will need one of everything. If we don't have an item, that list will also be included."

Two hours later, he was dressed again and sent to meet Restivo at the catapult; they loaded up and were launched for Pearl. He noticed that Restivo had received nine stitches to his face and was sporting a crisp Navy White enlisted uniform with a small canvas satchel. They were seated next to each other as the plane was loaded with mail, boxes, and dispatch cases. The launch nauseated them, but they both tamped it down and settled in.

"That will be quite a nasty scar," he said to Restivo.

"Yes, sir, it will. But it's a reminder that not every day is guaranteed. Besides, dames dig scars." Restivo grinned.

"But what if they don't?" Daniel asked.

"Then I'll find one who does."

"Good to know."

"Sir?"

"Yeah?"

"What's going on?"

"We are being flown to Pearl Harbor to meet with Admiral Chester Nimitz for a debriefing. This will be quite a whirlwind, so get some sleep if you can."

"Roger that." He leaned back, placed his cap over his eyes, and fell asleep within minutes. Daniel drifted off a short time later. When he awoke, they were on final approach. They landed without incident, disembarked, and were met by two Jeeps. They each climbed aboard a different one and were sent in opposite directions. A short while later, he was escorted to Nimitz's office, where two other Admirals and a court reporter with a dictation device greeted him; all were wearing whites.

He approached the hot seat and sat down. A small table beside him had a glass of water and enough space for his cover.

"What are you wearing?" asked Admiral Jenkins.

"A warrant officer's uniform," Daniel said.

"Why are you in it?" he asked sarcastically.

"Because Commodore King was so good as to provide me a uniform representing my rank and station," he replied.

"But it's Grey," said Jenkins with disdain.

"It's what I was provided with. I take it this was surplus because it's unpopular?"

Nimitz said, "Enough. We are here to listen to Warrant Officer Brevet Captain Cores' report on the Battle aboard the USS Aberdeen DD-351.7. Proceed in your own time and walk us through what happened. You have full liberty to speak freely."

This time was the same, with them stopping him occasionally to ask questions. Once he was done, the court reporter was dismissed. That's when the real questions started flying.

Admiral Jenkins fired the first volley. "What made you think you could just take command, and what were you doing on the bridge?"

"I was requested to the bridge by Mr. Begley. He was dying and gave me my battlefield commission. His final order was to "Fight the ship!" Daniel said incredulously. "Were you not listening to my testimony?"

"What? How dare you?" said Jenkins angrily.

Nimitz held up his hand, "Stop it, you two. We are here to get to the bottom of this, which doesn't help. But Warrant Core may speak freely. Continue. "

"What would you like to know?" he asked.

"How could you do what you did?" asked Nimitz.

"As I said before, I have a commercial captain's ticket," said Daniel tiredly.

"For a tugboat!" cut in Jenkins sharply.

"Yes, sir, but it's just a matter of scale. I have five years of experience running a 52-foot tugboat 15 feet wide. So, the destroyer is 377 feet long by 40 feet wide. Therefore, I had to allocate 7.25 times as long and 2.6 times as wide." said Daniel.

"Preposterous! You've never been trained the Navy way. You've never even been to college." thundered Jenkins, rising to his feet.

"And that's the kind of thinking that has us here today," replied Daniel defensively. "I was the Captain of a destroyer for 12 hours, and I saved the lives of over 200 servicemen, saved the Navy several million dollars, and at least eighteen months in the yards. I fought off the enemy, the fires, the elements, and the sea. I fired my guns and ran like hell for the atoll. You don't have to know much to do that other than how to steer."

"Jenkins, you need to shut up if you can't be civil," said Nimitz with a quiet but firm tone, "All right, we've been at this for hours. Let's break for lunch."

They got into Jeeps and cars, meeting at the O-Club, where they were immediately escorted in and taken to the backroom full of Burwood, which smelled of whiskey and cigars. A rather large table was set with fine china. There were finger bowls, and the first course was ambrosia salad. The second was ham steaks and Lima beans with rolls and rich creamy butter pats. Small talk and shop talk were happening, and Daniel could see this was a well-oiled staff machine Nimitz had. The dessert was bread pudding with raisins.

They retired to the veranda for brandy and cigars. Daniel sat on the wicker furniture, and Nimitz sat across from him with a snifter. "Quite a day, eh?" he asked.

He nodded, searching around him and not knowing what to say.

"You seem a quick study. We'll send you off to Officers Training shortly, then tactics, and finally to your following command. The whole process should take about six months. I was reading in your file that you struck for a warrant on the request of your Captain due to your Captains ticket. "

"Yes, sir," he replied.

"When you went to induction, did you tell them about the ticket?" asked Nimitz.

"Yes, sir, I did. I even showed them, but they didn't care because I didn't attend college. I wasn't from the right family. My grandfather had told me that the Navy is a giant machine, and I was just a tiny cog; to do what they told me, when they told me, how they told me, that my time would come."

"So, you were passed over?" he stated.

"No, sir. Ignored, not even given a chance to fail," he replied dejectedly.

"And now here we are," said Nimitz ruefully.

"Yes! Here we are."

"How many others are out there like you?"

"At least twenty," he replied quickly.

Nimitz choked on the brandy, "Damn! I thought that was rhetorical."

"No, sir. It's real," he said.

Nimitz motioned to a scribe who came forth and surrendered a legal pad. He pushed it forward with a pen and said, "I need names, ranks, and what we missed."

Daniel took the pad and started writing. Fifteen minutes later, he twisted it around to Nimitz. Who nodded and said, "Thanks, that's enough for today. He motioned to a Yeoman and said, "Set him up at the BOQ." The Bachelors' Officers Quarters was a hotel for unmarried officers on a temporary assignment.

He turned to Daniel and said, "We will reconvene tomorrow at 08:00. He will come to fetch you at 07:25. You are dismissed."

Daniel saluted, turned, and left.

# Cantonese Curses

In his room at the BOQ, Daniel was floored when he heard soft, female laughter echoing outside. He opened the frosted window overlooking the hotel's pool, and the most beautiful woman he had ever laid eyes on smiled up at him.

"Come on in. The water's just fine," she said, her perky voice reviving him after a tiring day.

Smiling back, he said, "Give me a minute." He searched through the kit, finding swim trunks and shower sandals before joining her at the pool.

Upon his arrival, she stood, and Daniel guessed she was just over 5 feet tall. She was dressed in a modest two-piece that showed off her long legs, and a flower was tucked into her black hair. She held two Coca-Colas and handed him one. "Hi! I'm Kim-Yee."

He grinned and replied, "Daniel Core."

"Oh really?" she raised an eyebrow. "What? No rank? I saw you in a grey uniform. What does that mean?"

"It's a work uniform introduced to the Navy by Admiral King. It's not very popular.

"Who gave you grief?" she asked.

"Admiral Jenkins," he said.

"Whoa!" she replied.

"Yeah, I know," he said, sitting on a chaise lounge. "So, what brings you to Pearl?"

"No fair. Answer mine first. What's your rank?"

"Warrant Officer."

"Are you in charge of Clerks or a typing pool?" she asked.

"No, I was in charge of a destroyer until yesterday."

"Then you're a Captain?"

"Not yet; just a Warrant Officer; you can be a ship's captain and not have the rank of Captain."

"Ah, yes. That's the Navy for you," Kim-Yee said. "How long will you be here for?"

"How about answer mine?"

"That's fair. I'm just a nurse."

"No, you're not; you are an intricate cog in a huge machine," he explained. "I heard you laughing before I came out here. What was so funny?"

"A parrot flew in, and someone had trained it to curse in Cantonese."

"Well, that's different since Hong Kong is several thousand miles away. Did you teach it to talk that way?" he asked half-mockingly.

"Why would you think it was me?"

"Because you are from Hong Kong."

"How did you know?"

"Accent mostly," he replied, dead serious.

"What accent?"

"You have a slight British accent. Also, your sentence structure is very proper."

"Oh, come on. You can't get all of that from a sentence or two?"

"Can't I? Am I right?"

"Well, your case is strong, but what are some other giveaways?"

"How do you say the last letter of the English Alphabet?"

"E-Zed."

"See."

"No, I don't."

"WE call it 'Z."

"Do you have any more examples?" She asked coyly.

Daniel reached across the table next to them and grabbed a small notepad and golf pencil. He wrote something down. "Pronounce this word."

"Aloominium."

He smirked, "We call it Aluminum."

"Okay, you win. That's a very talented set of ears that you have."

They continued chatting about nothing, trying to avoid discussing the war and its horrors. She finally asked him, "What are your plans for dinner?"

"I was just going to drop by the Chow Hall."

"You can't! Let's go out to someplace local," she said frankly.

"Sure. But I think it's too late to sign out a Jeep from the motor pool, and I just landed. Let me get over to disbursement and grab my pay," he said.

"Don't worry about it. My uncle has a Chinese Restaurant off base. We can eat there. I'll get ready. Meet me out front in an hour?"

"Sure." He scrambled back to his room to check his wallet and noticed a few 5-dollar bills with a note from the officers. *Here's some candy money. See the sights on us.* He kissed the wallet and said a thank you to the air like a prayer. This would be useful since his monthly pay was only $50 plus allowances. He freshened up and dressed quickly, buying a pack of gum, some postcards, and stamps from the front desk to pass the time.

The clerk told him, "Sir since you just got here and disbursement is closed, I can offer you a $5 advance on your payment if you need it."

"No thanks. But good to know." He waited, wondering what his monthly pay rate would now be, $350. He had never even considered it as he only ever spent about $15 a month, if that. He had about 40 minutes to spare, so he went to the dayroom and began writing to his mother.

Dear Mom,
All is well. I'm eating fine.
I just got promoted. I will be in touch.
With Love
Your Son,
Daniel.

He wanted to tell her so much more but couldn't. He couldn't even describe his meals to her, for they would be censored if he did. He still had time to spare, so he reached for a newspaper in the dayroom. He picked it up and read the St. Louis Star-Times from December 8, 1941, only about three weeks out of date. There was an ad for Brownie Jr. Cameras for $2.45, but the headline on page three caught his eye:

**"Troops And Police Guarding Vital Defense Points Here"**

Guarding Power Supply for Defense Plants here

Private Ray Steckler from Jefferson Barracks is standing guard at the Union Electric Co.'s substation entrance at 6441 Page Avenue, Wellington. Private Steckler would not reveal how many men were on guard at the station but said he and others from Jefferson Barracks arrived at 3 am. Today. (Star-Times Photo)

He heard a car horn honk and headed to the front door, dropping his mother's card in the letterbox.

A small two-seater sports car drove up with her behind the wheel. She was dressed smartly in pearls and a cream-colored mandarin dress that hugged her body. "You're kidding? Is that all you have?" she said incredulously.

"As I said, I just landed. I was debriefed, had lunch, checked in, and then met you," he replied, exasperated.

"Hop in. We must make a stop first," she said playfully.

He climbed in. She peeled out, heading for the front gate.

"Where are we going?" he asked.

"To my uncle's store."

"Why?"

"To get you a suit," she replied, shrugging her shoulders.

"Does he rent them?" he asked.

"No. He builds them."

"What about rationing?"

"He uses Gabardine for the pants, viscose and cotton blend for the shirts, and bamboo for the coats," she said, raising her voice above the engine.

"Must be expensive."

"No; $15 for all of it, including a tie."

They left the base, and he said, "Most places charge $22 for a suit and tie without the shirt. How does he do it?" he asked.

"It's a family business, and he's close to the base. It's all about location. Plus, he does Made-to-Measure, and your body is off the rack.

"That's the Navy for you," he replied.

They arrived, he was introduced, got measured, tried on a couple of different coats, and then chalk lines were drawn and pins inserted. He was amazed at how quickly the whole thing was done. He smirked, and she said, "What?"

"Well, this is the second time in as many days that I've been fitted for a suit in record time," he spoke. They boxed his uniform up with care. He reached for his wallet but was told that he had to sign a disbursement slip, and they would submit it to the Navy against his pay; he did, and they were on their way.

Daniel realized he was ravenous as they arrived at Chan's Chop Suey House. It was a white stucco building with a lovely Oriental Garden, and the aroma floating out made his mouth water.

Kim-Yee parked, and they went arm in arm up the walkway. Inside, they were seated quickly, and the waiter dropped off water, teacups, and a silver pot. She poured the tea, and he sipped it. The taste was remarkable.

"What is this?" he asked

"Tea, silly," she said coyly

"I know that, but what kind?"

"It's called Po-ley. It cuts the grease on Dim Sum," she said as her eyes widened. A three-tier stainless steel trundle cart was coming out of the kitchen. She waved it over excitedly.

"What's that?" he asked.

Some dishes were made of bamboo; others were small China plates with silver rings and a lid. In Chinese, she called out to the attendant. "Lo Mai Gai, Shu-Mai, Har-Gow, Fung Jeow."

"Hai," the attendant replied and placed the dishes on the table, grabbing a card and making several markings; they then pushed it down the aisle, calling out her offerings in a sing-song voice to the other guests. If they didn't understand her, she opened them up to look.

Daniel glanced down excitedly. "You will have to explain to me what this all is?"

"Chinese Food, Cantonese Breakfast, to be exact," she said, admiring the plates.

"Okay! What's with the Lilly pad?"

"That's Sticky Chinese Rice with duck and mushrooms plus mung beans," she said as she expertly used her chopsticks to unwrap the rice. The ceramic serving spoon was shaped like a boat, and she grabbed it to place some on his plate. He picked up his chopsticks and popped some in his mouth.

"Wow, that's pretty good; it reminds me of tamale," he remarked.

"What's that?"

"It's a Hispanic dish: a cooked corn cake made with pork wrapped in a leaf and steamed. I ate many of them while stationed in San Diego," he explained.

"Okay, so this one is a steamed shrimp dumpling," she said as she placed one on his plate. It was pale white and translucent, with the pink color peeking out, but she used her chopsticks to block his.

"Wait for it!" She smiled as she picked up a little spoon from a side ramekin that he hadn't noticed was on the table. There were several of them with silver covers. She placed a few drops of a red paste, followed it up with a dark black sauce, and mixed it with her chopsticks. She said, "Now dip it in that and try it." He did, and it was a new flavor profile. "Wow!" he said. "This is unlike anything I've ever had before. What's next?"

"This one is also made with shrimp, but it has ground pork and water chestnuts," she said as she placed it on his plate. To him, it looked like a Mallow cup made from meat.

"What's that yellow thing on the sides?"

"It's a wonton wrapper," she replied.

It went into his mouth after dipping in the sauce.

"That's pretty good, too!" he said, hiding his mouth with his hand. He put his chopsticks down, sipped some tea, and then picked them up again excitedly. "Okay, what's next on this adventure?"

She gave a naughty smile as she lifted the cover on the last dish. "Steamed and stewed chickens' feet!"

He reached out, grabbed one with the chopsticks, and laid it on the plate; steam poured off it.

Kim-Yee gave an approving nod. "Smart move. You might want to let that one cool off, or you could burn your whole mouth."

"Does this one need sauce?" he asked.

"No, it's got salted black beans. You might want to try it first and then add hot sauce if you think it's necessary," she said as she took her own from the dish and placed it on her plate.

He picked it up with the chopsticks and popped it in his mouth. He ate around the bones, used the chopsticks to remove them from his mouth, and placed them on the plate.

She looked over at him and put her chopsticks down a little roughly. "Oh, you've done this before!"

"Nope," he said, pleased with himself. "We eat turkey necks and smothered chicken over rice in Charleston. So, the principle is the same, minus the chopsticks."

"What's smothered chicken?" she asked quizzically.

"You take a whole chicken and cut it up into eight pieces. Then dip them in beaten raw eggs, dredge them in flour, and brown them in 1/2 cup of butter, oil, or pig fat in an iron skillet. Then chop up celery, onions, and garlic and sweat them."

"Sweat them?" she asked.

"Yeah, cook them until they are translucent. Then add a quart of chicken stock and 1/2 cup of flour, which you whisk in. Put the chicken back in the pot and cover. Cook over medium heat until it falls off the bone; it takes about 2 hours. Most of the bones are so soft that you can eat them. Serve over rice, and add salt and pepper to taste. Or some of this hot sauce."

The cart arrived again, this time with a different payload. She made several more choices, and the empty dishes were piled at the end of the table. She noticed him looking quizzically and said, "It's a way to verify the bill. Each dish has a different price, and we compare the total to the total number of dishes; keeps it fair."

"Ah! Good point. So, what do we have here?" he asked.

"We have a fried turnip cake with pieces of pork; then there's razor clams, another type of shrimp dish; this one is fried and rolled in tofu. And this, she said as she opened another sealed container that looked like little strips of bacon with odd ridges and black beans in a sauce covering it.

"Ah, chitlins," Daniel said excitedly.

"Chopped pork stomach with black beans," she said triumphantly.

"Yeah, we call them chitlins."

"You've had this before?"

"Well, not the Chinese way, but yes, several different ways, both American and Latino," he said.

"Okay, I give up! You are either an outstanding sport or a keeper," she said.

"Oh, was this some kind of test?" he asked.

"Well, yeah. Dating is just shopping for a mate," she said with a twinkle.

"How many other guys didn't cut?"

"22." she snapped off almost too quickly.

"Wow, what a torture test," he said proudly.

"It seemed to work and gave the proper results," she said coyly.

They ate more, and she showed him rolled beef crepes and stuffed eggplant with shrimp. The last to arrive were BBQ steamed buns and egg tarts. The bill came, and he reached for his wallet but was waived off by her uncle, who promptly tore it in two; he laid $2 down for a tip, and they left.

They went for a walk on the beach and drove back to base. He walked her to her room, and she gave him a look.

"Thanks for a nice time tonight," she said as she reached up and kissed him on the cheek. "I hope to see you tomorrow." She turned and walked into her room, shutting the door.

# But it's the Wrong Color

Daniel slept without dreaming and awoke very early to his phone ringing as the front desk gave him his wake-up call.

He was up, brushed his teeth, shaved, and went to his kit, where a Khaki Uniform awaited. He remembered turning his Grey inside out and hanging it on the coat rack.

He dressed and went to breakfast, then returned to the BOQ, where the Jeep promptly retrieved him, and he was back in Nimitz's office for round two.

Today was different. It was just the Admiral and himself, plus one scribe. The hot seat had been removed, and Nimitz was sitting on a green leather couch looming over a Continental breakfast of Croissants with jam, coffee, and fresh pineapple chunks. He had a folder in his lap. "Of the names you gave me, only 13 are still alive. Therefore, I've created a training cadre for y'all since we have enough. It's going to be fast and dirty. But I need y'all up to speed and in place quickly. I'm losing men in this war faster than I can replace them, and I'm mortified to be in this position. "

"Admiral?" He asked.

"Yes. Mortified because we... the Navy, messed up. We denied you your due. You're right. Y'all weren't passed over. You weren't even acknowledged. I'm correcting that and am implementing a full review of all jackets looking for people like you," he said around a bite of croissant.

"Thank you, sir; that means a lot to me. Where is this taking place?" Daniel asked.

"Treasure Island for Officer Candidate School; then back here for tactics. It will take a week or maybe two to get this entire program together, so you can choose to mend here or there," said Nimitz, washing it down with a gulp of coffee.

"What about Restivo?" he asked

"Who?" asked Nimitz.

"The witness I brought along," he said.

"Oh, the kid? He was given a Purple Heart and sent home on a war bond tour. I put you both in for medals, but they can take a while. He can return or enter recruitment or light duty until the war ends. It will be his choice. No pressure. That's very good. You are thinking of your men. That's the sign of a good Officer. I have a list of light readings for you. You can retrieve them from the quartermaster. You have a lot of catching up to do. You might not see me again. Who knows, but know this: I will always have your back and the backs of the others we failed. If you run into trouble or anyone else like Jenkins, I will come down on them like the Wrath of God! So, help me."

Daniel took the list, rose, nodded, and left. As he walked out, he scanned the list: The Naval Officers Guidebook, Janes Pocket Guide to Aircraft, Janes Ships of the Line, Napoleon's Military Maxims, The Art of War, Uniform Regulations United States Navy 1941, Military Table Manners, and Etiquette. "Light reading indeed."

After obtaining the books, he went to the BOQ's day room. He had lunch at the mess hall, then returned to his room to stretch out. He, unfortunately, hadn't seen Kim-Yee, but he had a lot on his plate. He had noticed that people tended to catch him when he wore his Khakis, and he was invisible in the Grays.

He walked over to disbursement to claim his pay and told the clerk to draw one month and send the remainder home. He was informed that he could only send one month's pay home, and they showed him the balance, and he choked.

His mind was reeling as he walked back to the BOQ, changed, and went to the pool, where Kim-Yee was napping on a chaise lounge. He went to the Coke machine, put a couple of nickels in, lifted the lid, popped off the tops with the opener on the side, and went over to her. He was smiling as he gazed down at her beautiful features. She woke up and thanked him as she took the soda.

"Well, you look worn out," he said.

"Wow, do you talk to all the girls that way?" she said mockingly.

He smiled as he could tell that she was joking. "So, how did you end up here in paradise?"

She shrugged, "Luck of the draw, I guess. Great weather, sun, sand, and surf; reminds me of Hong Kong," she said sadly.

"What's wrong?"

"Just work," she said.

"You need some cheering up," he told her.

"Oh, I know the girls are going to a Luau at the King Kamaya Maya Hotel. It would help if you came," she said excitedly.

"Sure, but I need to drop by the PX to get some civvies," he said.

"You seem to be ill-prepared for an officer," she remarked.

"Sorry, ma'am, but my belongings were destroyed when the ship was attacked," he said offhandedly and instantly regretted it.

Her face turned red, and her eyes widened. "I'm… I'm sorry," she stammered. "How many men did you lose?"

"Half of the ship's company, about 125, and all the officers," he said ruefully.

"Not all…" she started to say.

But he cut her off, "No! All," he said, his voice almost a whisper. He said as he collapsed into the chaise lounge. "I was battlefield promoted to Warrant and fought the ship."

"That sounds horrible," she said.

"It was. But I got the ship to safety. Put out the fires and fought off the enemy; then was flown directly here. It has been a whirlwind, so I don't even know what day it is."

She stood up, wrapped her arms around him from the back, and hugged him close. She stroked his hair, and a tear fell from her cheek as she could feel the raw emotion spilling out of him. She brushed it off and stood.

"Come on, enough of this!" she said as she grabbed his hand, and they got into her car and drove to the Postal Exchange, a military department store, where they picked up a Hawaiian shirt, sandals, sunglasses, and a hat. Then off to the Luau. They forgot about the war, drank Mai-Tais, ate pork and poi, and then took a cab back to the base because they had too much to drink. They repeated goodnight and went to their separate rooms. He fell asleep around 02:00. The next thing he knew, an insistent knocking was at his door. He answered it bleary-eyed and was greeted by the Admiral's aide wearing whites, all chipper and rattling off platitudes. He groaned and opened the door while he went to the bathroom to splash cold water on his face. Then he turned around and said, "I'm sorry you will have to run all of that by me again."

She harrumphed and said pointedly, "You will need to get dressed and report to Admin within the hour."

"Why?" he asked tiredly.

She blinked and looked taken aback, "Why to take your Captain's Exam, of course."

"I've already taken one," he said exhaustedly.

"That was the civilian exam. This is the naval one."

"Just like that?" he asked offhandedly.

"Just like what?" she shot back.

"Just like the Navy. Sink or swim; here's an anvil," he retorted.

She looked perplexed.

"It's not you. They just threw this at me," he said.

"But the test has been scheduled for weeks," she said incredulously.

"And I just found out. Let me guess, Admiral Jenkins is proctoring?" he asked.

"Yes?" she said, puzzled.

"Give me ten minutes. I'll meet you out front." He shooed her out, turned to his Wardrobe, and grinned. He showered and shaved in record time, then quickly donned his Grays. When he got out front, she was waiting with a paper bag and a cup of coffee.

"You can eat along the way," she said as she turned to look at him, going slack-jawed as she noticed his uniform. "What in God's name are you wearing?"

"It's a Warrant Officers Uniform!" he replied cheerfully, accepting the bag and cup.

"But it's the wrong color," she began.

"No. It's a work uniform," he said, scolding her.

"Don't you have anything else like Whites?"

"No. I do not because 4 or 5 days ago, I was a Gunners Mate first class. I know the order went out, but no one has given me an ETA on when to expect them. My khakis arrived yesterday, and it's Grey's turn." He smiled as he ate the bacon sandwich and drank coffee while they crossed the base. They arrived, and Admirals Nimitz and Jenkins were waiting for him on the steps. "You're nearly late," said Nimitz, pointing at his watch.

"That's what happens when you spring things on people," he retorted.

"Ah, don't worry. You've had two years to prep, and I know you know your stuff. This is to give us a baseline. So, we know which gaps to fill in your training," said Nimitz offhandedly. He glanced over his shoulder at Jenkins as he could feel the eyes boring into him. "What?" he asked sharply.

"He's out of uniform. The uniform of the day is whites," said Jenkins tartly.

"No, Admiral, I don't have them. I'm just a Warrant, and I know when I was fitted compliments of Admiral King that the order was placed, and I have not received an ETA. But you could put a blackboard up in the BOQ stating the Uniform of the Day because that info is supposed to be posted in a conspicuous and consistent place," he said, exasperated.

"You could have at least worn Khaki," shot Jenkins.

"Sorry, Admiral Jenkins, but they were worn yesterday, and the manual prescribes that each uniform should be given a day of rest between wearing and since I only have two. Today is this one's turn," he said smugly.

Nimitz smiled, and they turned and went inside the Admin Hall. There were rows and rows of desks, each with a glass of water, pencils, papers, sextants, and rulers. Plus, a big blue book on top with a plain white seal. He walked towards the lone empty desk and stood at attention. Admiral Jenkins told them to "Be seated." There was a loud sound as all of them took their seats.

"The exam will consist of several parts, each blocked out on your exam book. You may all break the main seal," Jenkins instructed.

They did, and he continued. "Each part of the test is timed. We will note that on the mainboard. We will ring a bell at three minutes, then each minute afterward. We will then call 'TIME' and expect you to stop and raise both hands. When we call 'Begin,' the process starts over. At the halfway mark, we will retire for 45 minutes for a bag lunch and bathroom break. 5 minutes prior, a bell will ring, and every minute after that, until the final call. Then, you are expected to be at your desk, ready to work. The doors will be locked until the exam is over. Good luck! You may begin."

The rest of the day flew by, and he noted that there were whole sections where he guessed like his other exam. But overall, he was confident that he had passed. Once released, he went with his fellows to the O-Club for a celebratory drink, then off to the chow hall for dinner. On his return to the BOQ, several messages were waiting for him. One stated that his Whites and the remainder of his officer's kit had been released and delivered to his room; another was from Admiral Nimitz congratulating him upon completing the exam and to report to his office first thing in the morning at 08:00 for a Continental Breakfast and debriefing. He groaned and showered and checked his uniforms. A note on his whites stated, "Do not wear until after commissioned." His Blues were acceptable and fit smartly. He was exhausted and noticed the bill from the tailors; he groaned and saw a letter slipped under his door while he was out. It was Vmail from his brother Stavros in the Army.

VM To: Daniel Core          From: Pvt Stavros Core
Destroyer USS Aberdeen       B.Co. 2-47 Inf. 3rd PLT
Pacific Fleet, Pearl Harbor   Leonard Wood, MO 65473

December 20, 1941

Hello brother,
Well, it finally happened. We are at war, and I can't let you have all the glory.
Sorry that it's taken me so long to write! So far, this is the third letter I've had
time to write since I've been here at Basic. The schedule here is insane, running
from 0430 hours to lights out at 2100 hrs. Mom has written back to me, but as
for Poppa? Who knows?
Life here isn't all that bad, now that I'm learning most of the ropes, but you live
in a constant state of paranoia & fear. It's mostly about figuring out what the
Drill Sgt. wants you to do and then doing it exactly, when & how he says to do
it. They encourage you to ask questions but keep you from knowing they want
you to get it the first time.
We'll be going to the gas chamber this week and will be getting to practice Basic
Rifle Marksmanship. For the most part, we've got the day off because it's
Sunday, so I'm using the little personal time I have to send letters while we clean
the barracks.
Hopefully, we'll regain our privileges in a week and leave this 'Total Control'
phase. It all depends on a few individuals learning to be self-disciplined and just
SHUT UP & STAND STILL! If we get our act together as a platoon (and I'm
guilty of a couple of mistakes myself at the beginning), we might get phone &
PX privileges back.
Well, I'm going to get off here and write Ristarnt
You take care and write me when you get the chance
Remember to put a big "3" on the envelope!
Your brother Stavros

Daniel finished reading the letter and chuckled as he remembered the shock and
awe of Basic training. He thought he would only remember some things that
they expected of him. It was quite a shock to go from civilian to sailor. But he
did it, and so would Stavros. He folded the letter up and placed it in his uniform
breast pocket. But he still was restless, so he showered, put on his pajamas, and

went to the day room to see if that newspaper from St. Louis was still there. It was, and he sat down to read.

## "KXOK Gave City Its First News of Japanese Attack

The first news of the Japanese attack was given to St. Louis by the Star-Times radio station KXOX. At precisely 29 minutes and 35 seconds after 1 pm yesterday, a National Broadcast Corps. The "Great Plays" program was interrupted while a KXOX announcer flashed this United Press Bulletin to the radio audience:
"WASHINGTON, December 7- The White House had just announced that the Japanese have bombed Pearl Harbor, Hawaii."
KXOX remained on the air throughout the night, giving its listeners up-to-the-minute news on the war."

"That's depressing; how about something else?" he muttered. He searched the paper for a more cheerful story and found it on page eleven.

## "Traffic Club To Hold Party For Children"

Three hundred underprivileged children will be guests of the Traffic Club at a dinner party on December 15 at Hotel Jefferson. After dinner, entertainment, clothing, toys, candy, nuts, and fruit will be provided. W.J. Ford is Chairman of the entertainment committee.

It was getting late, so he returned to his room, brushed his teeth, and went to bed.

# Gunpowder Tea

Around midnight, he awoke to a light tapping on his door. Groggily, he got up and answered. He was thankful he was wearing the BOQ robe; it was Kim-Yee. "Sorry to disturb you, but the moon is so large and full. It reminded me of Hong Kong so much that I wanted to share it with you."

He shook himself awake, slipped on his shoes, and followed her.

They walked along next to the pool. They stared at the moon and didn't say anything, just lost in the moment and enjoying the breeze. She leaned against him, and he put his arm around her. He noticed they fell into an easy rhythm around each other like they had known one another forever. "I guess this is what they mean by soul mates," he said softly to himself.

"Danny?"

"Yes," he responded.

"I like this," she said, almost purring.

"Me too," he replied.

"Where were you today?"

"Taking the Captain's Exam."

"Why? I thought you already were a Captain of a ship?" She asked, puzzled.

"For training purposes since my Warrant is not a Commission. They wanted to see what I know versus what I'm missing to create a training program in the future," he said.

"How much longer will you be here?" she asked.

"Less than ten days, but I will return after six weeks for tactics. Nimitz has something in mind for me and the rest of the training cadre. I'll meet with him first thing tomorrow to discuss where to go. I bet his staff is going apoplectic that I've talked to him more in the past two days than they have in the past two months," he said.

"Sounds like dangerous waters to navigate," she said lightly.

"That's the Navy." He yawned, feeling his jaw pop.

"I'm sorry," she said as she turned to look up at him.

"For what?"

"For disturbing your sleep."

"Nonsense, this is magical."

"I thought so, too," she leaned up and kissed him.

They hugged for a few minutes longer and returned to their rooms. He dropped into bed, and the next thing he knew, his phone was ringing.

He was up, showered, shaved, and changed into his khakis. There was Continental Breakfast at a nook in the day room. He grabbed a box of Kellogg's Corn Flakes and a chub of milk. He poured the cereal, added the milk, picked up the old newspaper, and began reading. He noticed a crossword puzzle named "Shooting Iron" with four different rifles pictured, so he started to work on it— horizontal 1. Three-letter word displayed a weapon. He looked to 2. down and saw it was a four-letter word. So, 1. Was 'GUN' and 2. It was 'Noon.'

He looked down at his watch and noticed the time; he downed a glass of orange juice, placed the tray in the nook, and exited the BOQ. His Jeep was waiting, and he was whisked to Nimitz's office. He arrived, was escorted in, and sat on the couch as directed by the Admiral, who waved him over.

Coffee was served, as well as croissants. He noticed more aides than usual in the office, and Jenkins sat beside Nimitz with a sour look.

"All right, Jenkins. Go ahead and say it," said Nimitz.

"Well," he said with an exasperated sigh, "You passed, but barely."

"Well, you don't look too smug about it," said Nimitz, looking at Daniel.

"Sir," he said. "That test blindsided me. But what do you want from me?"

"I want you to shine," said Nimitz.

"Well, I feel like I'm pissing in everyone's rice bowl," he retorted.

"Yeah, well fuck 'em'!" Nimitz said. "It's because of their incompetence that we are here now. Jenkins is mad at you because he feels that you shouldn't be in your position no matter what. No matter that we are at war and the needs of the service. He feels that I shouldn't be talking to you at all. What's this '*business*,'" he said sharply, "would be better handled by my subordinates! I am overseeing it personally and will continue to do so until complete." He looked darkly at Jenkins, who shrank a little at the rebuke. "But to answer your real question, I want to use the test to build the training program and as a yardstick to fit the candidates into their respective ships. It will be called V-6. Afterward, you will receive commissions according to your years of service, training, education, and experience. They will vary heavily from Warrant to Lt. Commander. Some of you will be dropped directly into XO positions; others will not. Most of you will command Liturgical vessels to send more officers to the front. You will backfill positions and work your way to the combat area. Some might never see combat; others will be in the thick of it. One caveat: your commissions are only for the duration of the war. And this whole process is experimental. Normally, it takes nine years of service plus a four-year degree to create a Captain. We don't have the time," he nodded to Jenkins, who began the debriefing.

"Let's go over what you missed and why. You didn't know the status of your bunkers nor the reserve fuel on a destroyer. Why not?" Jenkins asked.

"Because I was never given the information in the first place; plus, I know the consumption rate based on knots, and the temperature can affect efficiency," retorted Daniel. "You also failed to establish the parameters of your destroyer. Which class of vessel is it? Four stacks, two stacks? Coal-powered or diesel. Steam injection? Crew compliment? Total displacement regarding supplies and cargo? Peacetime fitting or wartime?"

The color drained from Jenkins's face as he realized these were valid points. Suddenly, he became less adversarial and genuinely wanted to understand why. He was not used to being questioned. He was used to making it so and everyone falling into lockstep. "All good points; you are correct. The parameters must be established because the test evaluates your critical thinking skills. Let's move on. You missed one asking about a plane."

"Same problem. What type of plane? Any passengers? What's the cargo? How many flight crew? Attitude? Fuel? Weather? Temperature? Flying in which direction? Into or away from a headwind?"

"All right. Got it," replied Jenkins.

The next few hours flew by, and they broke for lunch, but it was brought in— tuna salad sandwiches with fresh pineapple juice, water, lemonade, and coffee. Nimitz noticed that Jenkins was getting more excited as they dove deeper into the test. When they finally called it quits around 17:00, and Daniel was dismissed, he looked at Jenkins and said, "Well, go on...spit it out!"

Jenkins was very nervous and flustered, and he shuffled his papers and finally relented.

"Yes, Chester. Both you and his sponsor were right. We underestimated that young man. But he has all the qualities we look for in a Captain, and we have yet to give him a chance. We missed it. Twice!"

"Finally!" Nimitz said, slapping the armchair.

Jenkins got up to leave. "I'm going home now and taking tomorrow off."

"Well, you should since it's Sunday. Don't even bother to come in until 10:00 on Monday. I mean it. The whirlwind will still be here," he said, equally exhausted. Jenkins gave a half chuckle and left.

The next day was Sunday, and divine services were scheduled. Daniel donned his Blues and went with Kim-Yee to the local Presbyterian Church. She was wearing a red crinoline dress that flared out in all directions. The pearls around her neck matched the small, white handbag she carried. Afterward, they drove around and stopped at a roadside Tonkinese Restaurant. It wasn't nearly as lovely as the one her uncle owned, but it was clean, and the smells from the kitchen were wonderful.

Kim-Yee said when they entered, "I've never been here before. These people are not Chinese."

"I know," he responded. They are Tonkinese." The waiter arrived, and Daniel ordered in a strange-sounding dialect of what could be Chinese but with odd intonations, and Kim-Yee was confused.

"What did you order?" she asked.

He smirked and said, "You'll see."

Two green coconuts with the tops lopped off were brought out with umbrellas in them and glasses of water and hot tea. But this one was very different; it was black and smoky.

She looked at it hesitantly and asked," What is it?"

"Tea silly," he told her playfully, using the same tone she had on him last time the question was asked.

"Yes, but what kind?"

"Gunpowder," he said wickedly.

She tossed it back like a shot of whiskey and said, "Wow! That's pretty good." She tapped her index finger on the table a few times. "More!"

He reached for the pot and deftly served the tea.

The dishes arrived, and there was rice porridge, cold chicken, some rolls in clear rice paper with shrimp peeking out the ends, and a thin soup with meat and a plate of garnishes.

"Congee!" she squealed, clapping her hands together excitedly.

He smiled. "I'm sure you recognize the other dish, but what about the Pho?" He said, gesturing to the soup.

"I've never seen that before," she said.

"Great! Mission accomplished," he said as they dug in. He showed her the garnishes of lime wedges, Thai Basil, bean sprouts, cilantro, peanuts, and fish sauce. She experimented with adding them to the soup. She also used her chopsticks to grab a piece of meat and some rice noodles. She savored the complex tastes and happily said, "Mr., you've got some explaining to do."

"About what?" he asked innocently.

"About how you know that language and what to order," she said forcefully.

"I am a naval man and have spent two years on ships. I was stationed in the Gulf of Tonkin for six months. I can only count to ten, order a hotel room, a meal, drink, call a cab, ask for the police, and get to the hospital or ship. That's all," he said in a dignified manner.

"That's plenty," she said, smiling as she relished the meal.

They made small talk and finished up. He settled the bill, and they got back on the highway and just drove, enjoying the scenery and listening to the radio. An ad came on:

"If you lack Vitamin B1 and feel tired, pep less, get the tonic that says, "Let's GO!" SHERATON. Low-priced at your druggist. A Meyer Brothers Drug Company."

They snickered at the ad and were glad to be in each other's company. They stopped at a diner for a snack. He noticed the cigarette machine on the way in was stocked to the brim with Lucky Strikes, and only a handful of Kool's Menthol was left, which reminded him to get his ration when he next drew his pay. He had several months accumulated, and even though he didn't smoke, it was a great way to motivate people to do their jobs well and better than cash on ships.

"I think I'm going to order a slice of pie," he said.

"Me too, but can you add cheese to the top?"

The waitress looked a little confused but nodded. "We have several choices, Apple: Pecan, Chocolate, and Lemon Chess."

"I'll have pecan and a coffee," he said.

"I'll have an apple and milk," she said.

"What? No hot tea," he asked.

She smiled demurely, "Not with pie. I drank so much tea earlier that my stomach is sour."

The order arrived, and he noticed she had eaten her pie from the side. And she asked him, "Why do you eat it from top to bottom?"

"I don't know. Never thought of it.," he said, looking skyward for a couple of seconds, and retorted," Haven't got a clue. Why do you eat yours from the side and with cheese?"

"I don't know. That's all I've ever seen," she responded. "Do you want to try some?"

"Sure," he said, leaning forward for the bite from her fork. He closed his mouth and chewed; his face changed into a grimace as he swallowed. "NOPE," he said. "I don't like it, But thanks for the experience."

They talked some more, thinking of future restaurants and places they could visit. Though he didn't have a car, she told him it was okay to wait until he returned from Treasure Island. Otherwise, the cost would be prohibitive. They returned to the base and their respective rooms, but Daniel struggled to keep her from his mind even while alone.

The next day, he dedicated the entire morning to catching up with reading on the list Nimitz had given him. After a quick lunch, he did more homework until he thought his mind would collapse. A movie was playing on base, and he thought it might be a good reprieve. A newsreel announcer talked over the film of Russian soldiers taking emplacements with tanks in the background for support.

### "News Flash! Nazis Give Up Effort To Take Moscow Till Spring"

1. Dec. 8, (U.P.)-A Nazi military spokesman said tonight that Germany had abandoned attempts to capture Moscow for this winter. There will be no further advance on the Moscow front this winter...."

He had fallen asleep in the air-conditioned theater and was woken up by an usher; he couldn't even remember the movie. He exited the building and went by the chow hall; V-mail was waiting for him when he returned to the BOQ.

VM To: Daniel Core 1028185     From Ristarnt Core
  USS Aberdeen c/o Fleet Post Office     C.Co. 229th MI BN
  Pacific Fleet, Pearl Harbor     Box 1493
                                                 Presidio of Monterey, Ca

December 21, 1941

Hey brother, how are you doing? I hope everything is going well and you get everything you want from your job. I am very sorry I didn't have the opportunity to see you again. That's military life. Time seemed to slip away from me since it was not my own. But I was able to get with a buddy and go off base to record a letter to Mom. I know she'll get a kick out of hearing my voice. What amazing and terrible times we live in.

Soon, I will begin my voyage to Fort Huachuca, where I will again be under the rule of Drill Sergeants and the like. Hopefully, everything will work out quickly so I can get permanent duty to get out of the stupid training phase and begin to look forward to my time in the military slipping away. Nevertheless, I can still dream; at least, I think that is still authorized! Anyway, how is everything going? The last I heard was that you struck for Warrant and struck out. Working hard and having the right skills isn't enough? Is there nothing that can be done to speed up the process? More & more, it seems like the ones who are the most advanced in the military cause the most significant problems. Anyway, I read that Ft. Huachuca is 4800 feet above sea level, which will hurt since I'm used to running down here at a lower level.

Well, that's Taps,

Gotta Go,

With love, Ristarnt


Daniel finished reading and marveled at how the country's sons heeded the call to arms once they were at war. He folded the letter and placed it for safekeeping in his kit.

He saw Kim-Yee a few times more as the days flew by. Then, he got his orders to depart for the mainland. He settled the bill at the BOQ and asked if he could take the out-of-date paper with him, and they allowed it. Kim-Yee saw him off, waving frantically as the plane rose.

"On to the next chapter," he mused, smiling.

# Treasure Island

When the plane was on final approach, Daniel noticed that there seemed to be a shipwreck on the rocks on the shore. He disembarked and hopped into a waiting Jeep. He was taken to the main OCS building and shown to his quarters. There was a new kit plus running shoes and athletic wear. He changed into the day's uniform and sat at his desk looking at a list of books for the course, then grabbed a postcard and jotted out a quick note to Kim-Yee when a whistle rang out.

He leaped to his feet reflexively and heard the order to dress at his door. He stood at attention, and a Gunnery Sergeant was barking orders. They marched in formation to the mess hall, lined up at tables, and waited for the order to be seated. It was given. They sat and noticed that it had been set family-style. They were instructed to "Bow your heads and give thanks!" so they did. They were next required to "Serve the meal only!" The dishes were passed around, and when the last man had received his portion, the order was "Eat!"

They did, in silence.

The Gunny walked the line between the tables and said, "Gentlemen! Welcome to Officer Candidate School V-6. I am Gunnery Sergeant Fagot. This cadre is 'special.' We will be working with you 12-16 hours a day. There will be physical activities like running, calisthenics, and swimming. There will be outdoor activities like small craft boating, water safety, diving, and orienteering. Sound like a day at the Yacht Club?"

They all chuckled nervously.

"After that, we will have classroom training on military history, naval etiquette, math, calculus, and trigonometry. Sound like a day in college?"

They also chuckled at that.

"Every day here will be in the lap of luxury. Every meal is a banquet, every day an adventure! There will be torture tests when we are done with all of that. There will be rigors. There will be blood, sweat, and tears! Then, we will learn naval marksmanship and gunnery. Finally, the crucible! I will leave that one up to your imagination! Eat well and rest up because tomorrow, the fun at this resort begins," he finished with an evil laugh. "Tootle loo!" He strolled out of the mess hall.

They ate the meal of corned beef and cabbage with carrots, potatoes, and bread. There were pitchers of water, lemonade, and root beer. They had coffee, and the dessert was peach cobbler. Two other training sergeants were present and called out, "The meal is over! Stand too and prepare to March back to barracks. Shipley and Core, you have mess duty. March!"

They both stepped out of formation and started to clear the dishes. There was very little leftover, and they scrapped it into one serving dish for later disposal. He noticed a serving cart and nodded to Shipley, who retrieved it. They loaded it up and went to the kitchen. They washed the dishes, removed the trash, ensured everything was in place, and logged it onto the Kitchen Preparation Roster. They then reported to the chow hall where the other training sergeant was waiting, and he marched them back to quarters, told them softly to wash up, and hit the racks. After lights out, the barracks were lit with only a faint red glow. They could see a fire watch stander making the rounds. They showered quickly and hit the racks, passing out as soon as their heads hit the pillows.

The next day was basic all over again. Wake-up calls at 04:30 by a baton on the trash can. They were cleaning the squad bay, learning to dress in the officer's uniform. The different types of uniforms, the uniforms of the day. The why and the proud traditions of the Navy!

True to his word, Gunny Fagot did his level best to tire them out every morning. Breakfast consisted of pancakes, maple syrup, scrambled eggs, link and patty sausage, bacon, ham steaks, biscuits, jam, orange juice, milk, water, and coffee. As they were eating, Gunny Fagot walked down the line, "Gentlemen! It has come to my attention that there was some waste after last night's wonderful repast. The service does its best to keep you well-fed and has scientifically determined your caloric meal needs. Some of you disagreed with that determination. Now, the civilians must ration things that we take for granted. I don't like waste! Therefore, you will not leave the table until there is nothing left. You will eat your fill and then some. Are we clear?"

"Yes, Gunny!" They yelled in unison.

"Good! Now that we understand each other, you may continue. You have fifteen minutes," he said with an evil laugh as he walked out the double doors, whistling a jaunty tune.

They all looked at each other and, to a man, dug in deeply. When the time was up, he returned by exploding through the double doors, shouting, "On your feet!"

They complied, and he walked down the row, looking for something to yell about. He found it. He leaned down, gently tapped a plate with his riding crop, and cheerfully declared, "There's still a biscuit left!" he looked up at the closest recruit, "Workman?"

A hand shot out grabbed it and stuffed it into his mouth. He eyed the man across from Workman and said, "Fahit? What's that egg doing on your shirt? " Fahit stammered and was cut off by Gunny Fagot. "No matter. You two will have KP after we are done with our 5-mile run. Outside NOW!"

They ran and ran and ran some more, in the heat, in the rain, until someone threw up. Then the next man, and so on, until they were down by 50%. They stopped at a bog and were told by Gunny Fagot, "Y'all have done well and have earned a chance to cool off. So go cool off."

They ran to the water with green algae floating and dove in. After a few minutes, they were ordered to "Form up and resume March!"

When they returned to the squad Bay Area, they were told, "You all stink. Time for a shower!" And that was when they noticed that they were fire hoses brought forward. "LOCK, ARMS!"

They did, and the water was unleashed. After a few minutes, they were still on their feet, and the water stopped.

Gunny Fagot declared, "Good! You all can work together. Now, hit the showers and prepare for classroom training. You two report to KP!"

Every day was new torture. He was true to his word. There was blood, sweat, and tears. But they struggled through it, knowing that the pain was only temporary. On the run, one man tripped and fell hard. Daniel dropped back and helped him up. It was Fahit. He was a Filipino, very short, and very light. It was too awkward to prop him up over the shoulder, so he told him to climb on board, and Fahit wrapped his arms around Daniel and carried him on his back. He caught up, yelling, "Corpsman!"

They stopped, and a radio was pulled out. "Five minutes rest."

The Jeep arrived, and Fahit was sent back with a sprained ankle.

The Gunny was impressed. Daniel groaned as Fagot went on another rant. "Well, well. We have a real officer here looking out for your men. That's dedication! How many men have you commanded?"

"125!"

"125? Wow, that's a record! Where was this? High school football, a huge team?"

"No, Gunny. Half of the crew complement was killed in a destroyer I was serving on, including all the officers and boatswain." He said, exhausted and gasping for air.

"What did you do?"

"I took command per my orders from the last officer and the battlefield appointment from the captain."

"How could he do that if he was dead?" Gunny Fagot asked incredulously.

"The appointment was in the captain's safe. The last officer retrieved it, promoted me with a witness, and died," he said, not enjoying the attention.

"And what did you do then?" asked Gunny Fagot.

"I got replacements to the bridge and fought the fires and the ship. Got it to safe anchorage and reported to the Commodore," he said frankly.

"And then reported here?" he said, genuinely impressed.

"Yes, Gunny, but first, I reported to Pearl and Admiral Nimitz," he said sheepishly.

"Wow! And modest, too; when this is over, remind me to buy you a drink. Now resume MARCH!" he barked.

And so, it went on in a complete blur. As time passed, they ate, ran, shot weapons, took classes, and barely slept because there was KP, guard duty, fire watch, and the rest. There was not even a Sunday off. They had two hours for Devine service and then back at it. They were polishing brass, checking uniforms, cleaning weapons, and brushing up on anything they were weak on, knowing that the CRUCIBLE was looming. Not knowing what it was and dreading it all the same. He received a stack of mail. Some even had charred bits, so they must have been recovered from his former ship. The first was only an envelope from Mr. & Mrs. Joe Karnuta, who resides at 123 College Road, Pittsburg, Pennsylvania. He didn't know them, but they must have put a Christmas card in it. He wrote two letters to his mother and one to the kind couple.

VM To: Mr. & Mrs. Joe Karnuta          From Daniel Core
123 College Road                       4th Div. c/o Fleet Post Office
Pittsburg, Pennsylvania                San Francisco, CA

December 27, 1941

    To Mr. & Mrs. Joe Karnuta,
Thank you kindly for taking the time to write to me. Mail calls are always a joy;
you made the extra effort to get it here by Christmas. I'm on a training cycle
right now, so I won't be able to write back much, but I will drop you a letter
occasionally.
Regards
Daniel Core Warrant Officer


The last week arrived, and they were put into patrol boats and driven to the rock
formation jutting out into the bay. There it was. The ship that he had seen
beached. It was a complete Farragut destroyer in a semblance of dry dock as she
was lodged between two large rocks. They disembarked at the tiny port and were
given cards. Each one had a duty station listed and an expectation. They
scrambled aboard and were run through drills several times. Then, the real fun
began. He had noticed that there were lights and observation posts that
contained camera crews shooting film of the training up in the rocks.
Once night fell, the drills became more advanced, with natural fires being set
aboard the ship. They had to work together to fight the fires and rescue fallen
crew members. Halfway into the night, tracer fire struck the boat. Unbeknownst
to them, the ship had been rigged expertly with small explosives to simulate
incoming rounds, complete with broken glass. One rating was an amputee who
came staggering over with a realistic-looking wound. He took it all in stride.
They were told, "Clear from drill!" and marched to a mobile kitchen near a small
cave. They were given boxed meals and sat down for the first time in 10 hours.
Canteens of water were passed around and told to" Drink!" When that was
done, they were given another and told to "DRINK!" They were too tired to talk

and ate as fast as they could. Then, "Time!" was called, and everything started again.

They continued for 36 hours with short rest periods, generally two hours, just in time for a reset. Then it was over, and they were told, "This is the final exam! How you do will determine where you will be placed as well as your commission." They went up the scramble nets one last time and took positions. Daniel was amidship when a loud booming was heard that hurt his ears. The lights were killed, and scant emergency lighting popped up. He listened to the orders and felt the heat from the flames. The smoke was billowing in the passageway. It was thick and acrid. He ran over to the emergency box and grabbed a breathing mask. He also remembered to grab a flashlight and a red helmet. He donned the gloves, grabbed another, and passed it back. Whoever was behind him patted him on the back, and they both grabbed the fire hose and opened the hatch. The backdraft blew them nearly off their feet. They opened the valve, and heavy jets of water came roaring out. They tackled the fire with precision, checking each compartment. Once it was under control, they found an active phone and reported it. Then, the main speaker came to life. "Flooding in compartment 5! All damage control parties report. "

They ran forward, and a flood of water roared toward them as they rounded a corner. Grabbing the nearest railings, they held on as tightly as they could. They got to the watertight door control and sealed it off. Then, they activated the pumps and took control of them. Once the task had been completed, they called it in. They were then sent into the ship's bowels to retrieve wounded from engineering, and once they arrived, the watertight doors sealed them in. They had to figure a way out as the water was flooding in. They each grabbed a wounded man and the breathing apparatus and swam through a tunnel to safety. Even though they knew it was all a drill, it was so realistic that they kept their minds focused on the problems and solutions. Some were obvious, and others not so much.

Once he worked his way to the bridge, Daniel saw that it had been removed, and there were only jagged remnants. A man at the helm was barely hanging on, yelling through the wind whipping about them, "What are your orders, sir?" There was blood and entrails all over the deck. It was too real. He lurched forward and threw up. He then straightened up and spun about. "What hit us?" "Two torpedoes and a bomb!" said the Helmsman shakily.

He looked down and saw that it was Restivo at the helm. He did a double-take.

The rest was a blur, and he felt lightheaded when the whistle went off. A flare was sent into the air, and he heard the Announcement, "Clear from a drill!" He sank down the bulkhead and was teetering between passing out. Restivo was at his side. "Sir? Are you okay? Corpsman to the bridge!"

The Corpsman arrived, saw his face, and pulled out the smelling salts. They didn't work, and he gave in to the blackness.

He awoke in a hospital bed. Restivo was at his side. He shot up from the chair he had been sleeping in and called for a nurse. She came running and started checking his vitals. She gave him two salt tablets and a glass of water, then turned on her heels to get the Doctor.

"How long was I out?" he asked.

"Just a few hours," Restivo replied.

"How are you here?" he asked.

"Well, sir, after Pearl, I was given leave followed by a war bond tour. I was told that I could do that or return to duty. But I was not to be sent to a combat position since I was the only survivor on the bridge. I searched for something worthwhile, and the training film brigade looked promising." said Restivo.

"I need to get back to OCS," Daniel said suddenly.

The Doctor walked in and said, "Not so fast. Let me have a look at you." He searched for a pulse and timed it, announcing, "Well, you'll live." He smiled. "You were just exhausted. Too much work and not enough sleep. Plus, some shock as that CRUCIBLE is a nightmare!"

Restivo asked, "Can he go now?"

"What's the hurry?" asked the Doctor.

"OCS graduation.," said Restivo.

"Get him on his way then," the Doctor said, motioning them out with his clipboard.

Daniel grabbed his uniform and threw it on. They quickly left, and Restivo dropped him off back on base. Daniel ran to his quarters and began donning his dress uniform. He ensured everything was squared away and looked for everyone when he heard them return from lunch. They also donned their dress uniforms and went to the parade ground to receive their commissions.

True to his word, Admiral Nimitz was there shaking hands and being the master of ceremonies; then, it was Daniel's turn.

"Full Lieutenant Daniel Core," Nimitz called out.

His mind was reeling as most called were either warrants or ensigns; there had been one Lt. Junior Grade Bobby Fahit. Once complete, the families came down from the stands to congratulate them. He noticed Restivo and saw Kim-Yee. His face brightened, but he saw that she had a severe look.

Admiral Nimitz approached him and said, "Your wife hitched a ride with us."

"She's not my wife yet," he said, perplexed.

"Oh really? You might want to rectify that. She's quite the pistol when she gets her dander up," said Nimitz. "We'll talk later." As he turned to leave, she called out in tears.

"You barely wrote me." She sniffled.

Nimitz turned around and interjected, "Ma'am, that's my fault. I've been running him for 14 hours a day on average. He barely had any sleep and collapsed from exhaustion right as the CRUCIBLE ended. I'll see you both at the reception." He then turned and left.

Restivo waved and gave them some space.

"I'm sorry, my dear. I've been busy. But what's wrong? It can't be just that," he said earnestly.

She wiped tears from her eyes. "I've missed you. But I have something significant to tell you. I haven't been entirely honest with you."

He steered her towards the bleachers, and they sat.

"Haven't been honest? About what?" he asked, concerned.

"How old do you think I am?" she asked.

"Well, it's not polite to talk about a woman's age…" he began, but her frosty glare stopped him in his tracks.

"This is serious!" She said through clenched teeth.

"Woah! Slow down. I don't know, my age?" he started.

Her glare got worse.

He tried again, "25?" he asked sheepishly.

"No," she said fiercely.

"I don't know. And I don't know why it matters," he said, exasperated.

Her tone got even more severe. "It matters. It matters because I'm 15 years your senior."

He was surprised; he knew Asian women didn't show their age the same way as Americans, but he was still puzzled and said carefully, "Okay, and your point?"

"My point is that I'm too old to give you children; besides, I already have two. I'm sorry that I didn't tell you earlier. There was no good time, and I wasn't sure if you wanted a relationship, not with damaged goods." She trailed off.

"Damaged goods? What's that about? You were married before. Okay. You had a life before you met me. I get that. But why didn't you tell me about the children?" He asked, hurt.

She replied, her voice shaking, "Because I didn't want to scare you off."

"Preposterous! We just never got around to telling each other our life stories. We had fun. What's wrong with that?"

"Because I've missed you, and I don't want to go another day without you," she said, bursting into tears.

He held her in his arms, consoling her as she continued shaking. His mind was reeling, but he pulled her out to arm's length and used his hand to lift her chin. "Why are you crying?"

"Because you are a good man, you deserve your own children. It's too late for me," she said wistfully.

"Children are a blessing. If they come, they come. If they don't, they don't. But they are not a mandate for marriage."

"But what about my children?" She asked desperately.

"What about them? Why don't you tell me about them?"

"Well, my oldest is a girl, and her name is Hailey," she said, reaching into her purse and pulling out a photograph. It showed a girl about eight years of age who was the spitting image of her mother holding a small bundle. "And the little one is Jack."

"So, how old are they now?"

"She's now 11, and he's 3," she said.

"I can work with that," he said.

"So let me get this straight: you will raise another man's children?"

"No, my darling, I will help you raise a part of you. I want to spend the rest of my life with you, even with the war. I'm asking you to be my wife." With that, he kneeled, and from his pocket, he pulled out a handkerchief. It opened to reveal a tiny golden ring-shaped with two hands holding a heart. He had asked his mother to send this ring that belonged to his great aunt.

"What kind of ring is that?" she asked hesitantly.

"It's an Irish wedding band," he said. "Ahem...I need an answer," he said, looking up at her and smiling.

She nodded and burst into tears.

He stood and placed the ring on her finger. Restivo let out a whoop. Then stopped looking down at the ground. They laughed, and there was scattered applause from everyone else at the parade ground.

Restivo then pointed at his watch, and they followed him to the waiting Jeep. They went to the reception and did the meeting and greeting. Then dinner was served, followed by dancing.

As the night was ending, Nimitz took to the podium. "I want to thank each of you for helping make this class successful. You allowed us to shrink the training down from 12 weeks to 6. I'm allowing y'all three days' leave regarding that. But you must all report to the airfield 72 hours from now to pick up your orders and depart for Pearl. Good night."

# The Marriage

They left the party and went to the BOQ, to their separate rooms. Daniel showered, put on his pajamas, walked to the bar, and saw they had Old Grand-Dad Kentucky Straight Bourbon Whiskey. He poured two fingers into a glass and sat down to read the old newspaper. Even though it was outdated by a few months, he was missing out on snippets of life and needed the break. He glanced through it and realized there was too much news about the war, and he was sick of it.

Instead, he picked up a Life Magazine dated March 10, 1941, and let his mind wander. On page 29 was a picture of a chubby middle-aged man in a grocer's apron with a crowd around him near a produce bin. The caption read: New York's Extrovert Mayor LaGuardia put on a grocery store skit to explain the Federal Food Stamp Plan to his city's retail dealers. There were ads for cigarettes, liquor, DeSoto's, and Schlitz beer. The writing was bland, and he didn't think he was the planned audience for this magazine.

The next day, he and Kim-Yee ate breakfast at the chow hall. Then, they walked to the Administration Building to get permission to marry. To their surprise, the approval was already waiting for them. He chuckled. She gave him a questioning look.

"Last night," Daniel explained, "Admiral Nimitz addressed you as my wife, and I told him you weren't yet. So, he told me that I had better correct that error. It's good to be the king. How did you end up on the Admirals' plane?"

"I checked on the graduation date for V-6 and showed up at the terminal. They were in the lobby, and I asked if this was the flight to Treasure Island and that I was going there to meet you. Nimitz said, 'Hop aboard, Ma'am,' and that was that." She smiled, and they asked when and where they could get married today. They were told they needed two witnesses; he paid the license fee, then called Restivo and asked if he was free. He also contacted Bobby Fahit. They both said yes and agreed to meet at the Courthouse at noon. Then they went shopping for his ring. She said she didn't need another, and he found the perfect one. It was a simple Celtic knot made entirely of silver. Noon came, and they met up with Restivo and Fahit. The Judge was stern, and the ceremony went fast and smoothly.

They took a trolley car to Chinatown for a celebratory lunch. She introduced the other two to Dim Sum. She noticed that Restivo wasn't as adventurous and ordered Haw Fun- broad Chinese noodles with beef and green onions. He dug into it with Gusto, beaming from ear to ear.

The newlyweds said their goodbyes to Restivo and Bobby and began their tour around San Francisco to see the sights. They shopped for clothes and sundry items. Then, they checked into the Hotel Continental Honeymoon Suite. He carried her across the threshold, and she kissed him harder than ever before. They disrobed and took a long, hot shower together, slowly soaping each other up. After drying off, they fell into each other's arms in the bed. He was in ecstasy. They lay next to each other, basking in the afterglow. Their breathing was heavy; her hair was rumpled as well. The sheets were all twisted.

"Looks like we will need to shower again," he said as they returned to the bathroom.

They cleaned up, went downstairs to eat dinner, and discussed building their lives together. She asked to be seated in the garden section away from the smoking.

The waiter arrived with a bucket of Champagne. They waved him off, but he insisted. "Compliments of the Hotel because you are honeymooning here."

They thanked him, and Kim-Yee tried ordering a salad. Daniel said, "You better put 8 ounces of meat on top of that."

"Why? Can't a girl watch her weight," she said petulantly.

"Sure, but you can get smoked salmon, pickled herring, tuna fish, or chicken. Pick one," he said.

"Fine, give me the pickled herring," she said.

"I'll have the Prime Rib with a baked potato. And for appetizers, let's get the Oysters Rockefeller."

"What's that?" she asked.

He replied, "It's steamed oysters with watercress, bacon, cheese, and rock salt."

"I've never heard of it."

"Yeah, I ran across it when we stopped for Liberty in New Orleans," he said matter-of-factly.

"What else did you do on Liberty?" she said teasingly.

"Mostly, I would see the sights and try the local food. Take pictures and play chess in the parks."

"Why chess?" she asked.

"I don't know. Maybe because it's a game that has been around for thousands of years, and I can enjoy it with someone, even if I don't know their language," he stated.

"So, my darling, what are the plans?" she asked sweetly.

"Well, let's start with each other's life stories. I'm the fourth oldest of 13…." he started.

"13?" she said a little loudly.

"Yes, 13. I'm also a twin. There are three sets of twins: my brother Thanos and me, Theodosia, and my brother Stavros. Then there's Diana and Mercedes."

"That's many mouths to feed. But that's only half. Who are the rest?" she asked.

"From the top are my sister Midora, brother Ristarnt, or Richard. My twin Thanos, me then, my sister Theodosia, and my brother Stavros. Next is Antonio, sisters Revekka, Angelina, Diana, Despina, my brother Jason, and the baby Christos."

"Wow, you're Greek?" she asked.

"Yeah." he said, "How about you?"

"Wait, hold on a second. Your last name is Core. How is that Greek?" she asked, genuinely puzzled.

"Oh, my great-grandfather came to America and told them his name was Corenaphenos. They typed it up, but the ribbon ran out of ink, so only the first four letters were seen. He figured new country, so new name."

"I see," she said.

"Your turn," he said.

"Okay. I have an older brother, Alfred, a sister named Miranda, and another brother named Adam; then there's me and my little brother, Davy."

"Tell me about your husband. Did he die in the war?" he asked.

She looked away and said, "No. He seemed a nice man at first. He was my schoolteacher and about 12 years older than me. He scooped me up at 15, and we immigrated to America. We had a successful small Chinese restaurant, and I got pregnant with Hailey. He lost it and started yelling that I had ruined our future. He didn't like children. I had a routine pregnancy but was in labor for 32 hours, and they decided to go in and do a cesarean. Out came a perfect little girl, and he was disappointed. Saying, 'All of that trouble for a girl!' He started to resent me, and I could feel it. He treated me more like a student. I was never his equal. He had been to college, and I had not. He felt that he had rescued me from poverty and that I should be eternally grateful. Then, eight years later, I got pregnant for the final time. He was glad he had a son but said that now I had doomed us to a life of poverty, and coming here was to be rich and successful. He felt that I had torpedoed his future and that the children were a financial drain. I told him that the solution was to stay off me. He didn't like hearing that, and he struck me while I held our son. Luckily, when I fell, I turned and landed on my back. The wind knocked out of me, and I lay there gasping. He loomed over me with an evil glint in his eye. I was checking the baby, and luckily, he was fine. He was just scared, and he started crying. I had enough; I picked myself up and walked out the door. Hailey was at school, and I had my sister Miranda fetch her while I walked to the police station and filed a report. They took my statement and some pictures and went with us to pack some bags and ensure we were not harmed. We stayed at a hotel for several nights until he calmed down, then I went to nursing school, graduated, and the war broke out, and here we are." She finished tearfully.

"I'm sorry!" he said.

"Well, you asked," she said, exasperated.

"No. I'm sorry he could not see the value of you and the children. I'm sorry that he treated you all like objects and obligations.," he said fiercely.

"Well, now they are your obligations," she said a little tartly.

"And I'm gladly taking them on. I got three for the price of one. You did all the heavy lifting, and I'll help you finish up," he said, smiling.

"Don't joke," she told him with a dark look.

"I'm not. I'm elated." He beamed her a smile.

The oysters arrived, and they dove in. She liked them.

Then, a few minutes later, the main course came out. She liked the fact that the fish still had their heads. She also reached across, cut off a piece of his Prime Rib, and popped it into her mouth. "That's pretty good. I've never had that before!"

After they were done, coffee and tea were served, and out came a baked Alaska, a cake with ice cream on top, and a browned meringue over that. A sparkler was attached to the top.

After finishing the Champagne, Daniel, and Kim-Yee strolled to walk off the dinner before retiring to the room. They showered again and went to bed, noting that the sheets had been changed while they were out.

The following day, they had a breakfast of eggs benedict. Then, they went for a ferry ride around the bay. For lunch, he found a Siamese Restaurant where he ordered Pad Siam for her: an orange noodle dish that was slightly sweet, dusted with peanuts, and had cilantro, Siamese Basil, green onions, and scrambled eggs stir-fried then topped with chicken. He got Pad-Kee Mow, which she called "Drunken Noodles." They were broad noodles in brown gravy with sliced pork and were slightly spicy. They had Larb for an appetizer consisting of ground chicken blended with crushed water chestnuts and fish sauce. They also had hot tea, and he ordered a Siamese tea for her and got a Siamese coffee. Both came with sweetened condensed milk. Hers was served cold while he was hot. Dessert consisted of coconut rice with mango on top.

Then off to take more pictures and enjoy each other's company. Then they returned to the hotel and turned in for the night.

The following day, they took a cab back to Treasure Island, retrieved their bags, and boarded the next flight to Pearl. They arrived a day early, picked up his orders, and regained her car. She then drove him to meet up with her sister and the children.

It was around 16:00 when they arrived, and Miranda had afternoon tea waiting for them. She was older than Kim-Yee and a good deal thinner. She was dressed smartly in a blood-orange housecoat. He noticed the house was on a corner lot with lovely landscaping. It was a bungalow style with long wooden shutters and painted a cheerful yellow.

Little Hailey was in a white A-line dress with her hair braided in pigtails. Jack was wearing a sailor suit and wandering around the veranda as three-year-olds wanted to do.

Daniel walked up the stairs and noticed Hailey's discomfort. "Hello there, Hailey," he chirped. "Your mom has told me so much about you."

She looked up warily and said softly. "Hello, sir? Are you my new Pappa?"

He took a deep breath and said, as he sat down opposite. "No. I'll be your dad. Your Pappa is your Pappa."

He could see her visibly relaxing as the tea was served.

Jack came wandering over, saying, "Pappa? Pappa."

He looked down, said, "Hello, little one," and leaned down to pick him up. Jack squealed with joy.

He could see Hailey stiffening and feel the dark mood exuding from her.

'Wow, she's just like her mother,' he thought. Then she shot up and ran into the house.

He gave Jack to Kim-Yee and ran after her. She was sitting on the back stoop crying. He sat down next to her and said softly. "What's the matter, Hailey?"

"You don't want to know."

"I asked, didn't I," he replied thoughtfully.

"Well, I hate this dress! Auntie made me wear it."

"Then go pick another one," he said, puzzled.

"No!" she sobbed, "I hate all dresses!" She was blubbering.

"Then go get changed into something more comfortable," he said.

She stopped crying and looked up, her eyes wide with hope, "Do you mean that?"

"Of course, but if your school requires it and for church and functions that have it as a dress code; otherwise, you can wear what you want if it's decent. She grinned, jumped off the stoop, and ran to her room. She flew past Kim-Yee with boundless energy. His wife gave him a look, and he just shrugged.

Hailey emerged several minutes later wearing dungarees and a pale blue blouse with capped sleeves and white polka dots. Tennis shoes had replaced the Mary Janes, sporting a ball cap. Then she sat back down, and the tea service resumed. Miranda let Kim-Yee clear the dishes, and she stayed behind on the veranda with Daniel.

"Sir?" she started.

"It's just Daniel, sister. Or you can call me brother if you prefer," he said.

She smiled softly. Then continued, "Please be good to my sister."

"Oh. I will," he said.

"Never hurt her," she replied more forcefully than intended.

He raised an eyebrow and gave her a continuous motion with his hand.

She stopped. Then she said, "Her first husband was nasty to her. Hit her, made her feel stupid and no love."

"I know," he said, his face darkening. "I will never lay a hand on her in anger, nor the children, except for discipline."

"I can see it in your eyes. You will be good to all of them and for them. Your heart is full of love. I see how you look at each other, and I know this one will take a bullet for them," she said.

"As it should be," he said very seriously.

"As it must be," she finished. "Hailey, she good girl; not mad at you, her father-" She swore in Chinese. "-promises to come to pick her and Jack up for a visit.

Never show. She waits all day for him. Then you show up, just convenient target."

"I see. I knew there was a deeper reason because once I started talking to her, she seemed fine," he said, bringing the cup to his mouth and finishing the last of the tea.

He could hear both children giggling in the side yard playing tag.

"How do you know how to talk to her?" She asked.

"She's 11. I was once 11, but I come from a huge family, and Hailey is like my sister Theodosia." He gave her the rundown on his siblings. She nodded. He reached into his pocket and pulled out a ration booklet and a check. He handed both to her. "Since you run the household, here is my contribution."

She looked down at the check and said, "A thousand dollars?"

"Yes. Use it to buy a practical car the whole family can fit into."

"I don't have a license," she said.

"No matter; make the purchase and have them deliver it here. We'll worry about the license later. Oh, and don't pay more than $800 brand new with a full gas tank."

"But that still leaves $200. "she said incredulously.

"Yep, just use that for household expenses and let me know if you run low," he said as he turned and went towards the kitchen to help wash the dishes. They listened to the children playing and hugged each other.

Several hours later, they were seated at the dining room table.

"Hailey?" he said.

"Yes...sir?" she said hesitantly.

"We're indoors, so you must take your ball cap off. Also, did you wash your hands?" he said

"Oh hm...no......sir?" she replied, embarrassed.

"Then go take care of it. We'll wait," he said patiently.

She looked sidelong to her mother, who nodded. She harrumphed, pushed back from the table, and went to wash up. Two minutes later, she was seated, and dinner was served. It was a simple affair of soup with dumplings and cold chicken with Napa cabbage. Jack was in his highchair observing, and he cooed and babbled while he dug into his chicken and rice with a small silver spoon. There was very little talking going on, just eating. So, he started. "Hailey, how is school going?"

She stopped eating, looked at the ceiling thoughtfully, and said, "It's fine."

Kim-Yee said, "She is very good at Math and Science."

He continued, "I was terrible at Math but a whiz at Science."

"How could you be bad at Maths?" Hailey asked incredulously.

"Let's just say that it was a language that I didn't speak particularly well," he spoke.

"But you're a Naval Officer. It would help if you had Maths to drive a ship," she stated frankly.

"Hailey…" Kim-Yee said. But he held his hand up.

"Fair point, young lady; I didn't follow what they taught in school. It made no sense to me."

"Why not?" she asked.

So, smiling, he said, "'X' times 'Y' for the sake of 'I' because you say so is irrelevant."

She giggled, "That's absurd."

"You see my point," he said plainly

"Not really," she stated, still puzzled.

"If everything is a variable, then there is nothing to calculate. Parameters must be stated," he told her.

"I see," she said as she shrugged and returned to eating.

He looked over at Jack, who had fallen asleep in his chair. So, he rose and picked him up. He noticed Hailey was finished and excused her from the table. Kim-Yee and Miranda started to get up, but he told them to stay put by hand signal. He brushed the crumbs off the child and grabbed a dishcloth to wipe his face. He then walked towards the nursery. He found it quickly because he could smell the talcum powder.

He laid Jack down, removed his dirty clothing, and changed his diaper. Lastly, he lifted the child and placed him in the crib on his belly, using a small blanket to cover him. He felt her presence behind him, and she said, "You're good at that."

"I've had much practice," he said.

They returned to the table and talked about what had happened over the past few days, filling Miranda in on their honeymoon and the changes in the household. He asked about Hailey's school, friends, schedule, and the person she was.

Miranda said, "Hailey, good girl, smart but 'Aya,' head always in the clouds. Dreaming."

He replied, "Well, she is 11 years old. They should be dreamers."

Her mother replied, "Yes, but we expect more from her."

"How are her grades?" he asked.

They both replied, "All 'A's."

"Then what's the problem?" he asked incredulously.

His wife responded, "Simply making an 'A' is not enough. She must do better and achieve all 100s if she wants a better future."

"Let me stop you right there. I was an 'A-B' student. It made no difference to anyone what my grades were. The Merchant Marines and the Navy only cared that I had a diploma. Not that I made an 89 in science class. She is acting out because she wants to be a child. She is not stuck in her room working towards this impossible goal that is not hers."

Both ladies looked at him, and Kim-Yee replied, "Well, you are the master of the house…."

He cut her off, "No! We all have equal parts to play in this family. And you have both done an amazing job under difficult circumstances. I'm just here to help ease the burden."

He looked around the small bungalow and noted several repairs that would be necessary. Base housing did require that you keep it up and in good repair.

He could hear Hailey brushing her teeth, and then she came into the kitchen dressed in a flowery nightgown. "Good night, all!" she said and went to her room.

"It's late. Let's wash up and retire for the evening."

The dishes were done, and they both showered and put their nightclothes on. They went to the veranda and listened to the ocean waves, enjoying the breeze and watching the moon wax and wane.

The following day was a bustle as the household stirred and breakfast was made. Miranda was up early and had steamed pork buns waiting. There was cereal on the table and orange juice and coffee. Jack was in his highchair feasting on mush. He looked over everyone with a cheerful demeanor. Hailey skipped to the table and sat down. She was wearing dungarees and holding her sneakers and her ball cap. Her mother looked disappointed, "Hailey, why are you not dressed for school?"

"I am." She replied.

"That's not suitable." she began.

"It's not against the rules," she said, holding the school's handbook to her mother.

She took the book and looked through it, puzzled. "It must be in there somewhere...."

Hailey looked triumphant. "No, Mom, it's not there," she said, pouring cereal into her bowl.

Her mother found the page she wanted and began reading, "Young ladies are strongly encouraged to dress appropriately and keep their hygiene and appearance neat and clean."

Hailey countered, "It doesn't say I can't wear this. It doesn't even state what I have to wear." She said, adding milk and slices of banana. He noticed that these bananas were tiny, the size of two fingers, and came in a bundle that was two hand spans wide, and you had to cut them away and slice into the skin. You couldn't just peel them, and they were lovely and tasty.

"But Hailey, you look like a boy." her mother said, crushed. She looked to Daniel for support; he smiled and held his hands up in mock surrender.

A few minutes later, there was a knock at the door. Hailey leaped to her feet and said, "There's Miranda and Jill. Got to go; love you, bye!"

He called out." Love you too. Bye!" and laughed when he heard the screen door slam shut.

Kim-Yee popped him with a dishtowel. "Some husband you are. You're no help!"

"She's at that age," he said.

"What age?" both ladies asked at the same time.

"Double digits; the age of independence, this is where she starts to become her own person," he said.

Miranda thought about it and nodded. "Yes. Sis, you started acting like that, but only slightly. That was when you started playing basketball with the boys."

"Oh really?" Daniel said, "Do tell..."

Kim-Yee blushed and said, "It was not that big a deal. We just played basketball after school in a Public Park."

"It was a big deal. Sam had to follow you to make sure nothing happened to you." Miranda said in a big sisterly way.

"I was fine, and I see your point," she said.

"We've got to go. I need to report to Admin. Today will be a light day; I'm just filling out paperwork. I might be back for lunch." He said as he kissed her. He kissed Jack on the head, saying bye to Miranda before driving off.

He reported to Admin and was given a mountain of paperwork. There were his orders and dependencies to establish. New wills had to be drawn up. His children had to be added as his new heirs. His new rank and pay had to be adjusted in his jacket. He was about finished when Bobby Fahit walked out of an office. They waved at each other and met in the middle of the bullpen. They hugged and clapped each other on the back.

"When did you get in?" Daniel asked.

"This morning, and you?"

"Last night. It was a bit of a hard adjustment, but I think I'll live."

"Well, I'm off to the BOQ. Got to get some light reading done," he said, patting his valise. He handed the list to Daniel. It read: Naval Tactics and Coastal Defense, Fleet Tactics and Naval Operations, Fleet Tactics Theory and Practice, Examples, Conclusions, and Maxims of Modern Naval Tactics.

"Oye vey..." he said. "See you later."

"Bye," Fahit called back.

He looked at the schedule. It was reasonable. Mostly 09:00-17:00 Monday through Wednesday, with Thursday and Fridays set for 'Practical Practice,' and Saturday being optional makeup for weather, whatever that meant. But he was happy because it would give him time with his new little family. The outline for the class consisted of nine pillars:

1. Ships Organization
2. Engineering
3. Gunnery
4. Sound Gear Techniques
5. Attack doctrine and tactics
6. Escort- Patrol- Ship Handling
7. Ship Maintenance
8. Qualifications of the Naval Officer, by John Paul Jones
9. The Laws of the Navy by Captain Hopwood, R.N.

He went over to the Motor Pool and signed out a Jeep. It was a Bantam 3-seater, a small reconnaissance vehicle that only weighed 1,850 pounds and had multiple uses. The canvas top was stowed because of the excellent weather, and he had to put the windshield up. It drove a little rough but had extensive tires. He drove to the Quartermaster to retrieve his books for the course and cigarette rations, then went home. When he got there, Miranda was distraught, wringing her hands.

"What's wrong?" he asked as he placed his valise at the door.

"It's Hailey. The school called; she was fighting," she said pensively.

"Okay. Stay here and calm down. I'll take care of it," he said as he turned around and left.

He remembered seeing the school as he was driving across the base. He headed for it, accidentally taking a wrong turn because of one-way streets, causing him to be turned around. Finally, he made it, parked, and walked to the office. When he got there, he could see two girls on the bench outside. One was his daughter with a torn sleeve, ink stains, a black eye, and righteous indignation. The other was a taller girl with a crinoline dress, crying into a handkerchief. She had two bruises on her pretty face, and her left eye was swollen shut. She also had a split lower lip. Two other girls on another bench looked worse for wear. Their hair was messed up, grass stains on their socks, and one had dirt all over her face. They both looked mortified to be there and had their heads hanging low. But he also noticed wariness about them. He heard loud voices coming from the office. He stopped before Hailey and stooped down. "Did you start it?" He sighed.

"No.., but," she said quickly. He held up a finger. She stopped talking. The door was wrenched open, and a stern-looking woman in a severe grey dress that could only be described as a prison matron's uniform came out. He could see another woman behind her, the first girl's mother. She had a sneer that came from someone who comes from money or is very well-connected.

"Ah! You must be these urchins' stepfather!" she emphasized the last three syllables.

"Whoa there, Brude Hilda." he started.

"It's Hildegarde to you!" she spat, then said in a clipped tone, "Girls, March!" They hopped off the benches and strode into the office. All but Hailey looked mortified to be there. They lined up by the secretary's desk. He stepped past them into the principal's office. Both ladies followed him. Hildegarde closed the door and said sharply, "Ma'am, do not call my daughter an urchin."

"Well, the term fits. She showed up for school dressed like that," she said, holding her hand out and gesturing to his daughter. "We have a dress code, after all."

"I've seen it. Nowhere does it mention that dresses are required. It's very vague. It also does not state what is not allowed. So, she didn't break any rules. But you don't get a black eye from that."

"Yes, well. She assaulted my daughter?" Cut in the mom.

"And which one is yours?" he asked.

She was aghast.

"How about this?" he asked as he opened the door and entered the lineup. He snapped his fingers at the last child dressed in Gingham. "Name?"

She looked up and said meekly, "Meghan." then looked down again.

"Next.," he said.

"Margaret.," said the one sporting the dirt.

"You.," he said.

"Sally!" she said defiantly as she scoffed.

"Well, judging by attitude alone, I would say this one is yours," he said.

"Look what your daughter did to her." she cried.

"The question is what happened. It looks like three against one, and she took them all on. It's a simple case of bullying; let's get the story, Hailey; explain yourself."

She looked up and said, "I was working on Maths, and then Sally yanked on my hair. I told her to stop it."

"Okay, that's one. Continue."

Both women looked at him, not following.

"Then she put my pigtail in an ink well. Right as the bell for recess rang."

"That's two. Proceed," he said.

"I ran after her, and she called me a dirty…" she started, then quickly stopped.

"A what?" he asked gleefully.

"A dirty Jap!" she said, tears welling in her eyes.

Both women let out a gasp.

He looked at Sally and could see the cruelty in her eyes, and they sparkled when Hailey said the slur.

"I told her I'm Chinese, and she knows it!" She said, anger rising.

"Okay, then what?" he asked.

"Then she threw dirt at me and said I was a bastard of low breeding and that I should've been sent to an internment camp since I look like them."

"What did you do?" he asked.

"I slapped her," she replied.

"And?" he asked expectantly.

She sighed, "Then things went downhill from there." she trailed off.

He looked at Sally and said, "That true?"

She looked up defiantly and said, "Yes!"

He looked down the line, and the other two nodded. He turned around and said, "These two are just collateral damage. It's between our girls; can we leave them out ?"

"Agreed!" Hildegarde said and dismissed them. "Don't forget to wash up before returning to class."

They both stopped, turned around, and said, "Yes, mam!" in unison as they curtseyed.

The mom whirled anger in her face. "Why can't you teach your daughter not to act in a vulgar way?"

"Why can't you teach your daughter not to bite off more than she can chew? I can see that this has been happening for quite some time," he said.

"Don't you know who I am?" she asked.

"No, mam, we haven't been introduced. I'm Daniel Core, Hailey's dad," he told her flatly.

"I'm Captain Bridges' wife!" she said forcefully.

"Never heard of him. Is that supposed to impress me? Navy? Army? Marines? Air Corps?" he asked.

"Army," She snapped.

"Ma'am, I don't care. Your husband and I both have a rank that we've earned. Our children don't have rank. There is a pecking order, but it shouldn't be based on that."

Hildegarde cut in, "I can see that tempers are high. Let's step back into my office."

They followed her back in and sat down. Hildegarde steepled her fingers and began, "I don't see any reason for this to go on Sally's permanent record."

"I disagree." he cut in, "They were both active participants in the fight!"

"But their permanent records..." she said, holding her hand over her heart.

"Don't matter. When they graduate, a future employer will not call the school and ask about their deportment. They aren't going to say, 'Well, I can see here that you have all the right requirements for the job, but in fourth grade, you talked out of turn!' Do you see how ridiculous it sounds?"

They both nodded begrudgingly.

"Miss Hildegarde, what is the punishment for fighting?" he asked.

"Two days suspension up to expulsion," she admitted.

"And what do you think the girls deserve?" he asked.

"Well, I don't want to give them a vacation, but I must draw a line under it!" she said.

"What are you thinking?" he asked expectantly.

"Two days in-school suspension. They will do their work, but they also will have to work together performing chores around the school."

"I'm fine with that!" he said, hopping up to leave.

"Not so fast, Mr. Sit!" she said sharply.

She turned and said, "Mrs. Bridges, you may leave and take Sally. But I want both girls promptly at 5 am, and they will be here for 12 hours."

"Ouch! But fair," he said, spinning in his seat.

"Ahem, we are not done yet."

He slumped.

"We still have one matter to address," she said sternly.

"What is it, pray tell?" he asked.

"Her method of dress," she said.

"Hailey was up half the night looking through the book. It's not in there."

"Ah, here it is." She read him the exact quote that his wife had found.

"Ma'am, my wife read it to me this morning, and I looked through it, and it doesn't say what you can and can't wear. "

"Yes, it does. It says…" she started, but he cut her off.

"A suggestion is just that. It is not a rule. It's free to be ignored. Why don't you create a dress code listing what should and should not be worn? Until you do, she will wear what she wants if it's in good taste."

"But she looks like a ragamuffin," she said dejectedly.

"Her clothes were neat in appearance and in good repair before the fight."

"Mr. Core. You have a daughter, not a son." she started.

"I have one of each, Jacks only three," he said, slightly sharper than intended.

"Why would you let her dress in an unladylike manner?" she asked, perplexed.

"What so terrible about it?" he asked happily.

There was a light tapping, and the door opened slightly.

"Yes?" Hildegarde asked.

"Principal? May I go to the bathroom?" Hailey asked hesitantly.

"Of course, you may, but keep it brief and wash your face," she said tenderly.

Then, she whirled at Daniel and said, "Dressing that way is so vulgar. Do you want her to grow up to be deviant? A carny?" she said severely.

"My sister Theodosia dresses that way. She hates skirts and dresses," he said.

"What does she do now?" she asked.

"She works in a factory," he said plainly.

"Oh, dear. Well, I can see that you are new to fathering..." she started.

But he replied quickly, "Not exactly. I'm fourth in a line of 13 children, and I have a vast amount of experience."

"I see. If both girls can get along, I don't see why this must be included in their permanent records. So long as they abide by the terms, I will take your advice and see about the vagaries of our dress code."

"Thank you," he said and left. He waited in the hall for Hailey. She arrived, and they went out to the Jeep. He told her about the punishment, and she nodded. He told her he was taking her out for a snow cone because she defended herself. She was glad. Then they drove home. They walked inside, and he told her that her punishment at home would be not to play outside, watch her little brother, and wash the dishes. She looked taken aback but nodded.

"Great. Now watch Jack while Auntie and I go buy a car." He turned and said, "Miranda, let's go."

"But why now?" she asked.

"Because I will be swamped for the next several weeks and then deployed, this is probably the only chance I'll get," he said.

They went to the local Chrysler Dealership, and he picked out a Town & Country Wagon with wood paneling. The salesman followed him home, gave him the second set of keys, got into the chase car, and left. Once gone, Miranda went to give him his check back, but he stopped her and said, "That's for the household. Why didn't you deposit it?"

"I don't have a bank account. Always deal with cash or barter," she said, ashamed.

"Let's take care of that," he said. They loaded everyone up and went to the Navy Federal Credit Union. They opened an account and then went shopping for Hailey's school clothes. Then it was getting late, so he decided to drop by a Tonkinese takeout and grab some sandwiches, and he picked up a six-pack of Schlitz beer.

They were seated at the dining room table when Kim-Yee arrived. She looked exhausted and asked, "Whose cars are those outside?"

Then she saw Hailey's face, "What happened to you? Then she saw the ink stains in her hair and said, "I'm too tired!" as she slumped in the chair, "What's this?" she asked, looking down at the small French rolls. Jack held a slice in his chubby fingers and was gnawing at it. He held it out to his mother, and she just smiled and leaned down and kissed him. Miranda handed her a hot cup of tea, and she nodded thanks.

She took a long sip of the beverage and said, "Ah!"

"These are known as Bahn-Mi, a Tonkinese invention. They all start with French bread with butter and pate, a goose liver paste. Then pickled vegetables, like shredded carrots, Daikon, sliced cold meats, and cilantro, are added. Watch out for any green peppers. It's spicy."

"And you let the children eat them?" she asked incredulously.

"No, I had them make theirs without. They have a blue rubber band. All the ones with the red are spicy."

There was a knock at the door, and he could see it was Captain Bridges. "Be right there," he called out as he went to the icebox and grabbed two beers and an opener. He met the captain on the veranda and offered him a beer.

He accepted and started, "I would like to apologize for my wife's behavior to you. She's used to ruling the roost. And I wanted to check up on Hailey as I heard it was three-on-one."

"I think your daughter got the worst of it." he said, "The other two were collateral damage."

"Yeah, about what she said…" he started

"Yeah, about that…" he said curtly.

"I'm sorry. I thought I raised her better than that," he said, distressed.

"Well, then, it's something you need to correct. But that's an attitude adjustment; spanking will only go so far…" he said as he took a pull.

"Yeah. I see." he said as he drained the beer, "Thanks."

They shook hands, and he left.

He went back in just as Hailey was recounting the day's excitement.

His wife gave him a stern look as he sat back down. She looked at Hailey and said, "Off to the bath with you; soak well; I want all that ink out of your hair."

Hailey got up, went over to Daniel, and hugged him around his neck, pecking him on the cheek, "Thanks, Dad."

Miranda and Kim-Yee were stunned. "Well, that was fast!" she said, flabbergasted.

He just looked down at his sandwich and smiled.

"Okay. Now explain. "she said sharply.

"Explain what?" he asked.

"The car outside," she said.

"Oh, that." he waved offhandedly. "Well, we all won't fit into the two-seater..."

"How can we afford it?" she asked.

"Oh well. When I was breveted up in rank, they placed a large bonus in my pay. I double-checked with the disbursement, and it was correct. Since we needed a family car, I got that one. Also, we need to get a driving license for Miranda." he said.

"You can't keep spending money as you do," she replied.

"Hold on," he said, grabbing the checkbook off the counter and showing her the balance. Her eyes bulged at the amount, and she said, "We could buy a house with that much money.

He continued, "Miranda has $200 to run the household on. I bought Hailey replacement school clothes and dinner tonight. I only bought what was necessary. I spent it on the family. That's what it's for."

"Okay, fine, but home-cooked meals from now on." She said, tearing into the Bahn-mi with relish.

"Yeah, sure. It was just because there was so much to do. How was your day?" he said, relieved.

"Like you say. So much to do, I'd rather not think about it." she munched on the sandwich. "This is very good," she said, her mouth half full.

They heard heavy snoring, and they saw Jack pass out in his high chair, but this time, Miranda swooped in and grabbed the child, whisking him away. They just sat at the table and held hands, lost in thought. They heard the bathtub drain, and Hailey started brushing her teeth. Miranda could be heard scolding her in Chinese. They both just chuckled. He stood up, stretched, and said, "I've got to shower and hit the rack because Hailey and I need to be at the school at 05:00."

"Can you do that?" she asked.

"Yeah, because the first three days are classroom, we might get to the wet stuff. I'll know more tomorrow." He leaned down and kissed her. He pointed to the icebox where Hailey's restrictions about her chores and responsibilities were written in red pencil. Below it, she had signed it with the reason listed as "fighting at school."

She smiled and patted his hand, then focused on her tea.

# Combat & Tactics Training

Daniel woke Hailey up at 04:15 and got her ready. When they went to the kitchen, they found Miranda already there. She had packed a small brown bag with breakfast and gave him a thermos of coffee. He softly thanked her, and they left. He buckled Hailey into the Jeep, rolled it down the hill, and started it up. They arrived with fifteen minutes to spare and opened the bag. There were two Chinese bakery items. One was a hot dog wrapped in a croissant, and the other was a baked bun. He looked at the side and decided it was Chinese BBQ. "Which one do you want?"

She looked in the bag and said, "The hot dog," as she scooped it up. She started munching and found a smaller thermos that had milk in it. She opened it, and father and daughter poured the liquid into the cups, doubling as lids. They looked at each other and grinned. He saw the lights of two cars pull into the parking lot. Mrs. Bridges opened the door all bleary-eyed. She reached across the seat to wake up Sally.

Ms. Hildegarde arrived and said briskly, "Come along, girls, we have work to do," She took each child by the hand and walked them to the school. He smiled and heard Mrs. Bridges scoff at him. He just got into the seat and drove to the Admin Building.

He found the classroom he sought, set up in theater mode. He walked to the third row, sat down, pulled out his books, grabbed one randomly, and started reading. He had three hours or so to get acquainted with the subject matter. After reading 35 pages, he would switch texts. When the time had expired, he had noticed that the room was slowly filling up. There were about 50 students of all ranks and ages.

The instructor came in and announced, "Good morning. My name is Major Raphael Garrison. I am your instructor for the course. It will be on Naval Combat and Tactics. You are obviously in the wrong room if that information is new to you. Please correct that error." He paused, said, "Great," and then walked over and locked the door. "We have much ground to cover. But first, we need to get introductions out of the way. So, I want each one of you to stand up. State your name and rank, followed by your length of service and what type of vessel you served on." They each took their turn, but when they got to him, Major Garrison stopped and said, "I understand that you were serving on a destroyer as a gunner's mate when it was attacked, and all the officers were killed?"

He looked down at his feet and said, "Yes, sir." He was getting tired of telling the story repeatedly. But he did.

Major Garrison asked, "Have any of you heard this tale before?" A few hands shot up.

"Where did you hear it?" he asked.

"At OCS, a few weeks ago." Bobby Fahit said.

"Has any aspect of the story changed?" Major Garrison asked. He nodded at another student who said. "No, sir. He told it the same way both times."

"Why are you embarrassed by it, Mr. Core?" asked the Major.

"I'm not, sir! But other people lost their lives, and they did their part too. They should be remembered as well."

"And a reluctant hero at that. But my point is that information can change over time. Sometimes, it's a simple mistake to take down the information firsthand. Other times, it's when it's entered into the record or translated into another format or language. People don't know what you meant. They only know what you wrote. So, when you write your reports, always keep the tone correct and your comments brief and to the point. This will be a master's class in the subject, and the information here is classified as "Secret." You will review data as close to real-time as we can manage. We will be discussing naval formations and the latest battle doctrine. We will be covering naval battles from 1090 to 1914 in the text. Real-world events will supplement the rest. Brace yourselves; this will be a bumpy ride. We will have class Monday-Wednesday. It will be from 08:00-17:00. There will be a lunch break around noon for one hour. And two bathroom breaks as needed. On Thursday and Friday, we will have wet classes on various vessels. Saturday will be a makeup day. Sunday will be off for a day of rest and Divine Services. You are expected to be prompt, and I need your undivided attention. We will go very fast, and you will need to keep up. There will also be 30 pages of reading per text per day. Does everyone get that?"

"Aye, sir!" came the chorus from the students.

"Good, then let's begin. Our first foray into the topic will be the Battle of the Koyun Islands. Mr. Core, since you are Greek, you might know this one. Any input?"

"I'm sorry to say, sir. I've never heard of this one," he replied sheepishly.

"Well, that might be because it happened in 1090AD during the Byzantine Empire. But it was a remarkable feat by someone outclassed and overwhelmed yet still managed to stomp his opponent…. So, what are the best things to have to your advantage in a naval engagement?"

"The weather," a student called out.

"Yes, very good, but it can also be a great disadvantage," the Major said.

"What else? Mr. Deleganedis? We have few Greeks in here." Major Garrison said.

"The tide or current," Deleganedis replied.

The discussions about the finer points of coastal attacks and defense went on for hours. He knew that it was all-important in some way. He also knew they were taking a year's worth of classes from the Naval War College and collapsing it to the bare bones to keep with Nimitz's schedule. They were dismissed for lunch, and as he left the building, he heard a voice call out, "Pos Eisai?" (*How are you doing?*)

He half-turned and shot back, "Kala efcharisto." (*Fine, and you?*)

They shook hands, and Deleganedis switched to English. "I'm Thanos."

"Daniel. You know I have a twin brother named Thanos," he said as they continued to the Chow Hall.

"You're kidding?" he said incredulously.

"Nope," he said as they lined up. Today's menu was salmon patties with gravy over rice, tossed salad, bread, and peach cobbler for dessert. They also had sweet, iced tea available, so he knew the cook was from the South, and the smell made his mouth water. He smiled as he dug in. He heard Thanos choke a little as he drank the tea.

"A little sweet for you?" he teased.

"That's diabetes in a glass!"

"Hold on," he said and took his water glass, added the tea to it, and then handed it back.

He took a swig and replied, "Much better! How can you drink that stuff?" he asked.

"It's not that much sweeter than a Coke and a cola. But if you want to try something different, next time you're in the O-Club, ask for a Cheerwine from the bar," he said mysteriously.

"Okay," Thanos replied guardedly.

They devoured lunch and returned to class with five minutes to spare. Then on to round two.

Major Garrison started, "A central concept in modern naval fleet warfare is the battlespace: a zone around the flotilla where each ship performs their duties correctly. The P.T. boats aim to screen the task force and attack targets under the direction of the Commodore or Admiral. The Minesweeper is there to detect and engage threats before they become dangerous to the convoy. The destroyer screens the larger ships like battleships and aircraft carriers. The cruisers are there to run down detected enemies and support the larger vessels. The battlecruiser is the last line of defense in this arrangement. Of course, all this works in concert to see the enemy without being detected. Therefore, submarines and aircraft are also included in the detection bubble. Open water is the best location for a fleet as the land's topography can help the enemy determine precisely where a fleet might anchor and place itself in a field of Naval Battle since the draft of each type of ship is known.

Also, these ships are essential to protect the various other types of support vessels like oilers, colliers, tankers, tenders, ammunition, rescue, and hospital ships," he droned on, and even though Daniel was interested, his mind was wandering. The next thing he knew, it was time to go home. They were dismissed early so he could run by the school and retrieve Hailey.

When he pulled up, she was coming out, and he could see how tired she was. She lifted her hand and barely waved. The drive home was silent as Hailey was too exhausted to continue any conversation. She went into the house, dragging herself, and headed straight for the bathroom. He heard the tub filling up. Miranda gave him a look, and he just shrugged. Little Jack came wandering up, saying, "Poppa?" Daniel leaned down and picked him up, kissing his cheek. Jack cooed at the attention and beamed. He sat at the kitchen table and bounced Jack in his lap. Then, he smelled the delicious aroma that was all around him. He should have noticed it when he entered but was so tired that he didn't.

"What's that wonderful smell?" he asked Miranda.

She smiled and said, "Mushrooms, big Chinese Oyster kind. Then Egg Fu Young and Chinese Broccoli."

"Sounds wonderful." he said, "And how was your day?"

"Me? Oh fine. Jack has too much energy. Can't keep up," she replied, bustling around in the kitchen, checking the dishes and tending to the fire. He got up and took Jack into the living room to run around. But Jack climbed up into his lap. The next thing he knew, he was asleep, and his wife shook his shoulder.

"Time for dinner, dear," she said.

He felt the drool and wiped it off his cheek. He looked down, and Jack was asleep in his arms, snoring lightly. She picked him up and carried him away. Daniel got up and walked to the table where a sumptuous meal awaited. Hailey was already seated in her nightgown. His wife came to the table and started filling bowls with rice and passing them around. The dishes' lids were removed, and the chopsticks began flying. He noticed Hailey had a fork and knife by her place setting but didn't need it. She reached over, picked up the flat little fried omelet, and placed it in her rice bowl. Then she grabbed an oyster mushroom and looked around for something.

"What is it, Hailey?" he asked.

"Where's the gravy? She asked hesitantly.

"Hailey, we don't use gravy on egg fu young." said her mother gracefully.

"Well, you might not, but I do," she said.

"But Hailey, that's an Americanism." her mother said.

"And I'm an American! I was born here, right?" she was starting to get defiant.

"Hailey, your Auntie has been cooking all day. Making gravy for one serving does not make sense."

"Well, I, for one, would like gravy as well," Daniel said.

"Aya!" his wife said in answer.

So, he told Hailey, "I guess that's a no, kiddo." shrugging.

Her face fell, and she looked down dejectedly.

"How about we add ketchup?" he said, his eyes gleaming with mischief.

Her eyes lit up as well as she grinned and said, "Well, I don't know?"

"It's an omelet," he said reasonably.

"I'll try it.," she said, reaching for the condiment bottle on the table.

His wife slammed her chopsticks down and said, "AYA! I'll make some."

Five minutes later, father and daughter were smiling as the light brown gravy was heaped over their egg fu young.

"You spoil her," she said after Hailey brushed her teeth.

"Not really. She's just coming into her own. It's normal and natural. You've just never experienced it. I have multiple times with my siblings," he said.

"How was class?" She asked.

"Fine, just a lot of Naval history with battles back to 1090 A.D.," he said, "How was your day?"

She walked over to the icebox, grabbed a beer, popped the lid, and took a long pull.

"That bad?"

"Yep, but we have nothing stronger in the house." She sighed.

"I can pick up some whiskey," he said.

"Sure. Let's also get some sherry and Chinese cooking wine while we're at it."

"No problem, but what's been bothering you? You seem more reserved," he said, concern in his voice.

She brushed it off, "It's just… we seem to have a lot of young men that come through that are maimed for life. It's horrible, and I know they received first aid and general care from the hospital ships, so they are just receiving follow-up care. But it's tragic! All those young lives wasted," she said in a melancholy mood.

"Well, my dear. We either fight them over there, or we fight them over here. I was here when they attacked the harbor. It was ghastly."

"I know. I had just finished nursing school the day before in Hilo, and the attack came. We heard the air raid sirens go off and saw the smoke rising. We headed to the airfield and were flown in for triage. The battle was raging all around us, and we went to work. There were so many broken bodies, too many to cover with blankets. We were told to retrieve the blankets for the living and flip the bodies face down for grave services to identify them later. How about you?" she asked wearily.

"I was asleep when the attack came. We were berthed next to the Missoula; we fired up the boilers and started shooting planes down. We fought to the harbor entrance and took out a sub. Then got out to open sea, escorting others to clear the bay and set up a cordon waiting for an attack that never came."

She finished her beer, and they kissed Hailey good night, showered, and went to bed.

The following day, he awoke to the smell of coffee and congee. He dressed and went to Hailey's room, but she was not there. She was seated at the kitchen table, finishing up a bowl. Miranda handed him a cup of coffee, and he thanked her, then grabbed some toast and added jam. He ate quickly, trundled to the Bantam, and went to the school.

After dropping Hailey off, he headed to his regular classroom, where he found a note pinned to the door. 'Lecture in War Room 4.' He realized it was a much larger room with many telephones. There was a sizeable glass-topped table in the center, many tiny model ships, and large sticks with flat dowels on the ends. He sat down and started reading. The next thing he knew, the class began, and the door was locked.

Major Garrison said, "I could tell that many of you were distracted because I threw too much info at you yesterday, so we have some visual aids today."

A voice said, "Major, why is an Army officer teaching the course?"

"Oh, that's easy because the Corps of Discovery helped to map the rivers and coastal waterways that the Corps of Engineers took over. We also have boats. Any more questions?" he waited a moment and then began again, "Here you can see the coastline off the aisle of Lesbos...."

They looked down at the map, which was lit up from underneath. When he shifted to the Battle of Red Cliffs in China, he punched a button, and a pulley system moved the map as it was changed over. They were impressed. This style of teaching helped immensely. Now, he could see what the Major was talking about.

"Remember that the orders will come from the Commodore, and if you have information that would cause a conflict in those orders, make sure to relay that to him because you may have a different line of sight. But the decision is theirs. You must follow orders. Period. Especially in a war, your job is to gather information and relay said report so they can make better-informed decisions. Take the Battle of the Java Sea that transpired just a few days ago; it was called ABDACOM, an acronym for American-British-Dutch Australian Command. Three main problems crippled this command.

First, they integrated sailors from four countries and three different navies who spoke other languages. Secondly, they needed more airpower, which hampered intelligence gathering. Thirdly, any mechanical breakdowns meant that if they could retire for repairs, it would be Surabaya, the main target for air attacks by the Japanese, or the floating dry-dock at Tjiltap, which is on the southern coast. If the ships were severely injured, they were to be scuttled. The defense force for the area only consisted of fourteen warships. There was Strike Force 10 for the immediate defense, which consisted of the heavy cruisers HMS Exeter and USS Houston; light cruisers Hr. De Ruyter, Hr. Ms. Java and HMAS Perth; and destroyers HMS Electra, HMS Encounter, HMS Jupiter, Hr. MS. Korteaner, Hr.MS Witt de With, USS John D. Edwards, USS Alden, USS John Ford, and USS John Paul Jones."

"Wait for a second, wasn't Core on an old four-stacker?" asked Thanos.

"I was on a two stacker, and we kept it running. But why don't we let the lecture continue? I had a line of sight to only a small part of how they operate. Then we can comment," Daniel said to the room, and they murmured in agreement.

The lecture continued, "Spotter aircraft was low on fuel when it caught sight of 56 troop transports headed to the west of Java with warship escorts, and 41 transports were sent to the eastern end. Admiral Doorman was ordered to 'Attack the enemy until they are destroyed.' The hope was to send the meager defense force to meet and take out the Japanese convoy, return to base, and then rearm and sortie out again to pound the second convoy. After two days of searching, Admiral Doorman went out to sweep for these attackers but was still looking for them. His superior was angered at his lack of results, and his reply was, 'Let me know where they are, and I will engage them!' Unfortunately, the crews were at the point of exhaustion as they had been at Battle Stations almost nonstop for two days, so he decided to return to base, and he was spotted by Japanese aircraft when he made his about-face turn.

When the defenders were attacked, they wandered into a minefield. They engaged two destroyer flotillas, six destroyers under the command of Rear Admiral Nishimura Shoji, whose flagship was the light cruiser Naka; eight more destroyers were under the control of Rear Admiral Tanaka Raizo, plus three heavy cruisers under Rear Admiral Takagi. The Defender's ships were all built in the interim period between both world wars, with their construction being between 1920 and 1939. So, they could have been in better repair, but most had upgraded their coms and radar to current specs, and half had removed their forward torpedo tubes among the U.S. ships. This would play in the battle, not for the best outcomes. Also, the ships built in the interim period did not have the best watertight control doors as they did not go all the way to the top, so they were prone to flooding completely, which was adequate if you were trying to drown out a fire but could cause you to lose the ship. The USS Houston was the best armed of the flotilla, with nine 8-inch guns in three groups. Still, after her section of guns had taken a hit and could not track effectively, thus reducing her effectiveness by a third since she could not be repaired on sight and should not have been pressed into service, it was all they had to throw at the enemy. One of the main problems for this flotilla was the TBS devices because as they fired their main guns, they would knock out the TBS radios and cracked their landing lights, so handheld lights were used to signal back and forth between ships. They kept hearing the Japanese floatplanes spying on them, dropping magnesium flares to let the enemy convoy know where to engage them. Does anyone know the best tactics for fighting ship to ship at night?"

Daniel replied, "Sending starburst shells."

"Correct. But explain how that works to the class, please," said Major Garrison. "First, you must have a target, then load a starburst shell and fire it along its trajectory. This will illuminate the target well enough to be seen by other guns, and they can zero in on it and hopefully destroy it," he explained.

"Excellent. But the shells fired on this case fell short and failed to backlight it. Also, the torpedoes used came from the Japanese destroyers and not a submarine, as was thought by the flotilla. This was called the Type 93 or Long Lance, and it had an even greater range than anyone thought. The firing between forces was slow for two reasons: not having a line of sight, and they had been at it for over seven hours. The Ally's ammunition was dwindling, and they had less than 50 rounds per gun available when suddenly the Japanese stopped firing. It took a minute to figure this out, and once it was realized, Doorman ordered all ships into a hard 90-degree turn to starboard because the Japanese had launched torpedoes. This tactic was used before in other engagements, and all in the battle line began their turns. This tactic was called combing the torpedo to turn into a course that would parallel the torpedo and present a narrower profile, attempting to mitigate any hits. This echelon turn caused all the ships to head East, but the Java would never complete her turn as word had been passed via handheld lamps from the flagship to each ship. Some had working TBS, and others did not, so the lines of communication took a few minutes to execute, and that caused the Java to be hit as her time had run out.

At 23:32, she was struck on her port bow by one of eight torpedoes launched ten minutes prior. Her aged design would show poor internal compartmentalization and an obsolete gun layout. Shortly after the explosion, a second came, and lookouts reported seeing bodies flying from the ship. There was a huge fireball, and the Perth reported feeling the shockwave. Once the smoke cleared, it was determined that the second explosion came from her aft magazine, where extra ammunition was being stored. The ship began listing to one side, and there was no chance to launch the lifeboats. Most life jackets were gone in the explosion, so crew members threw anything that would float into the water and jumped in. The Perth rescued those in the water and only managed to pull 19 from the sea out of a total complement of 528. Admiral Doorman ordered the column to form around him, and they did as they were completing their final turns to go back into formation.

Then, another long-lance torpedo hit the DeReyer. She lost power as her turbines were compromised. This started a fire that spread with extraordinary speed, and everything aft of the catapult was in flames. The ammunition for the Antiaircraft guns immediately began cooking off, and an oil tank had ruptured and leaked bunker fuel into and outside the ship. Because the turbines were knocked out, there was no water to fight the fire. Then the fire spread to the pyrotechnics locker, and all of it went up in a strange fireworks display. The ship was doomed. Now, what have we learned from this?"

Fahit said, "Always have a backup plan and an alternate rendezvous point."

"That's very good," said Major Garrison, "What else."

"Make sure that you have at least three to four different types of communication available, and all are conversant in it," said a midshipman.

"Good! What else?"

Daniel said, "Always expect the unexpected and plan for that."

They spent the next several hours analyzing the engagement, replaying all the forces' maneuvers, and determining why they did what they did and if any mistakes were made. Was it crew exhaustion? Poor information? Late information? Bad weather? Bad luck?

The following two days flew by, and he was reporting to the bay for Waterworks training. They were loaded up on P.T. boats, and each had a turn at the helm, commanding them. They were told to take them through their paces, and they raced around the harbor, shooting past buoys and crisscrossing each other's paths. He knew they were being evaluated every step of the way. The P.T. boats attacked a column of ships and fired dummy torpedoes. The fronts were loaded with red dye, and the tips were leather. He was able to get two hits on a cruiser. When they returned to the docks, they saw the rest of the P.T. boats were already tied up, and the crews were milling about. He tied up as well, and they disembarked.

A tall officer named Coleman came looming up to him and said in a menacing tone, "Why didn't you save some for the rest of us?"

"What?" he said incredulously.

"Here you are, hogging all the glory."

"I was going through paces as we were trained. Everyone had an ample turn at attacks."

"You little shit." He took a swing.

But Daniel was not there. He had reflexively sidestepped.

"Stand still," he grunted as he threw another punch.

Major Garrison yelled," What in tarnation is happening here?"

Daniel turned and said, "Nothing, sir; he disagreed about his poor seamanship and equally poor targeting as he couldn't get a hit on the Cruiser and was jealous of me."

The Major nodded and said in a mischievous tone. "Well, we can't have that, so why don't we go over to the boathouse and settle this."

They drifted over, and once they entered, they saw an official boxing ring set up. Major Garrison went to the center of the ring and tossed them a pair of three-pound gloves.

Daniel looked down at them and asked, "Are these even legal?"

"Nope, but they do make a statement. Now, each of you goes to your respective corners and wraps up. You have two minutes."

So, he stripped down to his waist and donned the gloves. Fahit was wrapping the gauze material around his wrists and tucked them in. He said, "You got this. That man's a blowhard and the schoolyard bully."

The bell was wrung, and Coleman came out swinging. But Daniel just danced out of his way. Down came another blow, but once again, he wasn't there. The crowd groaned as they wanted to see a fight, and someone yelled, "Quit dancing around and get on with it!"

So, he entered striking distance and let a haymaker and an uppercut fly. Both hit Coleman squarely in the face. He retreated to let him get his bearings. Coleman shook it off and came charging in wildly and reigning down blows. But Daniel's guard was up to protect his face, and he took a few blows to the body. Then Daniel swung four times in succession, two jabs to the body and two uppercuts. Coleman went down on one knee, tried to shake it off, and then held up his hand in surrender. Major Garrison said, "Time!" and the bell was wrung. Daniel helped him to his feet, and Coleman begrudgingly let him as he was too dazed to do anything. A towel was tossed his way, and he used it to help wipe down Coleman, who was sweating profusely. Two of his comrades came up and took him away.

Major Garrison said, "That was some nice footwork out there. You could have taken him with the first punch. Why didn't you?"

"He knows he was outclassed because he had to work for it. If I only threw one punch and he woke up two hours later, he would convince himself that I had cheated somehow, which would be ongoing. This way, he had skin in the game and lost. No more wounded pride, at least I hope so."

"Smart!"

"Well, pappa told me never to start a fight but always finish them. You don't even have to win. Just make it so expensive that they don't want to tangle with you again." He dressed, went to the Bantam, and drove home. They went around the harbor on tugboats the following day and spent time docking them and pushing barges in and out of positions. Then, after lunch, they were sent to the fireboats. When the time was called, they were all weary.

"That's all for this week. See you all on Monday." Major Garrison called as he left the Pier, talking to the evaluators.

Daniel got into the Bantam and raced home. He was thinking of all that was covered this week. So far, he has had 20 hours of antisubmarine instruction, three hours of medical knowledge, eight hours of seamanship and ship handling, seven hours of communication, radar and navigation, gunnery drills, communication or command procedures, and three written exams.

When he arrived, Jack was on the porch playing with blocks and studying them with an intensity rare in a three-year-old. Hailey was squinting at a book and rubbing her eyes. They both looked up and smiled as they saw him. He walked up the stairs, and she ran to hug him. Jack wandered over, tugging at his trousers. He leaned over and picked him up. Then he sat on the veranda couch and asked them about their day. Jack retrieved his blocks and brought them to him, beaming as he showed them off. Hailey chatted about school and an upcoming carnival. She kept rubbing her eyes; he noticed they were red and asked her about it.

She shrugged and said it was nothing but asked him for some aspirin for a headache. He agreed and went inside to get her St. Joseph's chewable. He came back out with the bottle and a glass of water. She took two pills, tossed them back, and followed the water, draining it in one pull. He told her, "Whoa, their sport. They are chewable."

"Oh, sorry, I thought you were giving me grown-up aspirin," she said frankly.

"Why would I do that?" he asked quizzically.

"Why wouldn't you," she asked pensively.

"It has to do with dosage and strength. Your body is developing, and your liver and organs are 1/3 the size of adults. If I gave you adult aspirin, it could harm you."

He heard Miranda scream and saw black smoke roiling out the front door. The children visibly jumped at the sound.

"Stay here!" he ordered and ran inside. Miranda was recoiling from the stove, and he saw the source of the fire, which was hot oil. He grabbed the bucket of sand and yelled, "Out of the way!" and threw the sand. He then grabbed a cover and threw it on top. They were both coughing, and he turned to her and asked, "Are you hurt?"

She fell into a chair and said, "No sir…just my pride. I ruined dinner!"

He surveyed the damage and saw she was right. "That's okay. Just help me open all the windows to air out the house. Then we are going out to dinner. I'll tell Kim-Yee to meet us at the Officer's Club. He told Hailey they were going to the Officer's Club and that she would have to wear a dress if she wanted to go. She relented because the girls at school were constantly regaling her about the club's food and atmosphere. They piled into the wagon and drove over to the O-Club. They arrived and parked the car, then strode up the steps and signed in. They were seated, and he ordered a whiskey sour. There was a light buffet set up since it was Happy Hour. Miranda took Hailey over to the buffet, and he watched Jack, who stood up and leaned over the table, finding the breadsticks and happily munching away.

He smiled at the chance to relax finally. A waiter arrived with a phone, and he thanked him. "Hey, honey. No. No. Just come over to the O-Club, and I'll explain. It was just a minor kitchen mishap. See you soon. Love you."

Ten minutes later, the girls came back, and Miranda had two cocktail wieners on her plate, whereas Hailey had several, and her aunt scolded her in Chinese. He heard the squealing of tires and knew it was Kim-Yee pulling in. He turned, saw her explode through the doors, and held her hand to the greeter, waving him off. He stood and smiled sheepishly. She strode up to him, ensuring everyone was okay and physically relaxed. So, she sat down, grabbed his drink, and tossed it back. Then, he stood up and took him by his arm to the buffet. She grabbed a plate and passed him one. "What happened?" she asked as she heaped the appetizers on.

"Just a minor mishap in the kitchen," he told her.

"How minor?" she asked.

"Just a bucket of sand," he replied.

She turned to the end, where glasses of red wine were set up, and grabbed one. He followed. When they returned to the table and sat down, she asked her sister in Cantonese what had happened.

Miranda replied, explaining that it was only a cooking oil fire, but no one was hurt- except her pride.

Kim-Yee nodded, picked up a morsel, and brought it to her mouth. She bit down on it with a satisfying crunch. "What am I eating?" she asked.

"Those are called crostini. That one was tomato, Basil, and Cheese. The next is sliced sardines, and the other is Prosciutto bacon."

"And the wine?" she asked, taking a sip.

"Chianti.", he told her.

"It's sweet," she said, smacking her lips.

The waiter arrived with a cart that had two silver trays. "The chef has sent out these two dishes for your children." He expertly removed the covers and exposed a fancy version of a hamburger he had placed in front of Hailey. Her eyes were wide with childlike glee, and he pulled a booster seat for Jack. To Jack's annoyance, Daniel lifted the child and put him in the chair. Then, a napkin was tucked under Jack's chin, and the cover was removed, showing a small bowl of white rice and scrambled eggs. Jack beamed with pleasure, picked up his spoon, and shoveled it into his mouth. The waiter leaned over and whispered into Daniels's ear. "The Maître De wishes to see you."

"Sure," he said and stood up. He followed him to the front. The Maître de informed him that only one or two guests are permitted even though he is an officer.

"That's fine. But my wife is also an officer, so we are good."

"No worries. But we need you to fill out a signature card with your military identification number. Here is a card for your wife as well. We have waived the annual fee because you are active military, but you must eat at least two meals here per month. Otherwise, you will be billed anyway."

"That sounds reasonable," he remarked.

"We have a lovely brunch planned on Sunday." The Maître D said.

"Thanks. I'll ask her," he said as he left and returned to his table.

"What was that about?" she asked quizzically.

"Just some paperwork; I had to fill out a signature card with my military identification. Here is yours." He said, handing her the card.

"Why?" she asked, perplexed.

"Because it is a club, and they must bill us for services rendered."

"Can't we pay cash?" she asked.

"Of course, but if we don't eat there at least twice a month, they will charge us for two dinners anyway," he said. "I'm sorry about all this. I wanted to take you here for dinner with just the two of us," he said dejectedly.

"But there aren't just two of us. It's a package deal, and you've done wonderfully," she said, kissing him on the cheek. Both children stopped and looked at them, then at each other. Then, both shrugged and continued eating. Miranda got up and got a second helping. She returned with several small pastries and a little plate of something else. "What is this?" she asked.

"Oh, that's nice. It's called Shepherd's Pie. It's an Irish dish with ground meat, onions, and mixed vegetables with mashed potatoes. It's a casserole."

She slid her fork into it and gingerly took a bite. "Tastes pretty good but needs hot sauce. Is it hard to make?" his wife asked.

"Nope; it takes 10 minutes to cook on the stove and 30 minutes in the oven. The kids like it," he said as she gave them each a bite.

"I'll remember that," she said frankly.

"I just remembered we need some Worcestershire sauce," he said, snapping his left two fingers together.

"What's that?" she asked.

"An American version of soy sauce," he said. "It's needed for the dish."

They finished up when the coffee service arrived on a cart with eclairs. Hailey brightened until she saw her mother cut it into thirds, which she portioned to Miranda and her. She didn't say anything, but she knew not to push her luck.

He got up to go to the bathroom when Nimitz waylaid him. He put his arm around him and asked, "Hey, how are things going?"

"Fine," he replied.

"That's a cute little family you got there. I want you to take 21 days' leave when the training ends. Go home to Charleston and show them off to your mom. Make some memories." Then his face got serious, "Because I'm sending you into the dragons' teeth." He saw Kim-Yee brush a stray hair from her face, and his face lit up with recognition.

He steered Daniel back to the table and said, "I thought you looked familiar; you're that nurse who gave me a dressing down on my first day at Pearl. It's been bothering me since that flight to the OCS graduation."

She replied, "I thought you let me on the flight because of before."

"No. I didn't because you were in a dress uniform. You dropped his name, and I said, 'Hop aboard.' But I had too much to do and was surrounded by my aids. I am sorry about that." he said regretfully.

"I'm lost. You two seem to have a history," said Daniel.

"Just a working relationship," she said, her face reddish from the attention.

"Do tell," he said, intrigued. "I was only here for the last part. I don't know the whole tale."

"I don't like to brag," she started.

"It's not bragging if it's true," encouraged Nimitz as he finished his drink and ordered another one.

"Okay," she began…

# Kim-Yee and the Admiral

"I had just graduated from nursing school. All the boards and tests were over. We got our results back and celebrated. It was December 6th. The next day, we were scheduled to fly from Hilo to Pearl and tour the big hospital." Kim-Yee took a sip from her coffee and grimaced. She tried adding sugar, but it wasn't to her liking, so she flagged down a waiter and asked for hot tea. Then she began again.

******

She had woken to air raid sirens going off. They all stumbled out of their bunks and began to automatically don their uniforms, knowing that some disaster had happened. They spilled out into the quad and heard the drone of aircraft. A bus pulled into the courtyard with an Army Sergeant wearing a sidearm at the wheel. He opened the door and said, "Pearl Harbor is under attack! Get on board if you want to help; we have a mail plane waiting."

The mother superior nodded and hurried them on board. "Go with God, my children. I will pray for your safety."

He drove like a madman, stopping short of the runway, went to the rear, and grabbed crates, and he and another soldier started loading them. They hurried aboard and found nowhere to sit, just heaps and mail sacks. They scrambled over them and dodged the crates being loaded. The hatch shut, and there were two sharp clangs against it, letting the pilot know to take off. He was very young, and his voice trembled as he leaned back and yelled, "Hang on. This is going to be grim!"

Amber, one of the other nurses, could be heard reciting the rosary. They could not see anything outside because this was a cargo plane with no windows. Only the forward windscreen allowed any visual. The pilot gunned the engines and shot forward right to the cliff's edge. Her stomach lurched as the plane dipped and then slowly climbed. They could see massive dots in the sky.

The pilot called out, "Those are not our planes. All the aircraft carriers are out to sea. I can hear one of y'all praying back there. You might want to say it louder because if they see us, we're toast!"

Someone started openly weeping, and she called out in a harsh whisper, "Silence! It doesn't help! Keep it together! When we land, it will be in a combat setting; we must move fast to get out of here. He will barely have time to stop."

The next few minutes dragged by, and the silence was excruciating. The pilot started the final approach. "Brace yourselves for an emergency landing! I'll roll to a stop! Y'all jump out and run for the nearest hanger or cover. I'll taxi to safety."

They came in hot and heavy and saw two American planes on their wings providing cover.

"Angels six and seven, I have 25 guardians on approach. Tell the hospital they are on their way. The tower is not responding."

"Tower personnel are dead! Stay on the approach five by five. We got you," a male voice said. He was very calm, and then he yelled, "Break right! Do not circle. Land hard. Now!"

The pilot obeyed, making the sign of the cross. They slammed into the tarmac, bouncing and swaying to an abrupt stop. They threw the hatch open and started pouring out. Kim-Yee was counting and came up one short. The pilot was the last out, shoving her forward.

"Where's Gwen?" she yelled.

He yanked her along, screaming, "She's gone! Head for the hanger."

"What?" she yelled in shock, "How?"

"Broken neck!" He slung her to the left as bullets screamed past where they were just a heartbeat ago. They fell into sandbags, and he rolled to the right and headed for a locker. He grabbed a wrench and hammered away until it popped open. He grabbed a BAR-Browning Automatic Rifle and some ammunition, then announced, "Ladies, we made it this far, but those white uniforms are making y'all targets. Change into some coveralls out of the lockers. There are three medical kits in each hanger. One is small and red. That one has morphine. The rest are large and white. I'll find us a ride." He went over to a table with a small radio and turned the dial. He picked up a headset and announced to the fighters that covered their approach, "Angels six and seven, thanks for the assist, 24 guardians safe and sound; one KIA."

"Name of KIA?" another voice that identified itself as a backup from the tower questioned.

"Gwen," he said and hung up.

He searched the drawer, looking for keys.

One of the nurses, Le'le, shouted, "Found it," proudly jangling them in her hands.

"Good. Let's load up three or four of y'all on this fire truck. We will go out there and grab as many wounded as possible. Then, bring them back here for triage. I need one of y'all to operate the radio."

Kim-Yee called out, "Becky, radio. Stacey, Alana, and Megan load up. Le'le, you're driving." She felt confident in the choices as Le'le's father ran a trucking company. Becky was a Western Union operator before, and the rest had the highest marks in their classes for trauma.

"Kehlani, you're in charge of triage. The rest of you search for med kits for the hangers and other aircraft." She clapped her hands together and shouted, "Get moving NOW!" She loaded herself into the passenger seat, slapped the door twice, and Le'le put it in gear, and they shot off into the fray.

The truck careened onto the tarmac, Le'le dodging left and right to avoid being the target of incoming rounds. They came upon a small group of soldiers and sailors firing at aircraft. All were wounded, but they waved them off. A Gunnery Sergeant yelled, "We're still in the fight! Go help others." He pointed to another sandbag emplacement where they saw a wounded man trying to apply a tourniquet. They drove over, and Alana and Megan jumped off and went into action. She got out, and she and Stacey grabbed a stretcher and loaded him onto it. They got him into the bed between them, and she grabbed the red medkit and ran over to a crashed plane. The tail section was separated, but the gunner banged away at the retreating aircraft. She ran to him and yelled, "Where are you injured?"

He continued firing the double-barreled 50-caliber machine gun and called, "Shoulder!"

She grabbed a styrete of morphine, jabbed him in the leg, and then pinned the tag to the trousers. The gun barrels were bright red, and he

ran out of ammo and turned around to let her bandage him up. Once complete, he opened some more cans and started banging away.

She turned and went on to the next wounded. Once full, they roared across the tarmac back to the hanger. They kept the pace up for hours. They didn't have time to think. Just stabilize, get to triage, and load up the ambulances.

When things calmed down, they grabbed a Jeep and went to their crashed plane, where they grabbed the crates of medical supplies. They got back just as a truck arrived, and they loaded up and were shuttled over to the hospital. The wounded were pouring in from Battleship Row; many were burned badly, and both they and the supplies were dropped off on the lawn. At least they had the foresight to move their Caduceus badges to their collars, so there was no question they were nurses.

After several more hours of brutal triage, they were exhausted. A female officer named Gates had approached them as they were scrubbing up. "Girls, thank you very much. I can see that you are all in quite a state. We will go over to the quartermaster and draw fresh uniforms and toiletries. Then to the chow hall, and by the time we are done with that, we should have bunking arrangements made."

They wearily followed her to a waiting truck and went to the chow hall, which served a simple stew over rice. There was bread and jam but no butter. Lemonade, milk, and coffee were available. All ate mechanically, and then they marched over to the quartermaster for a uniform draw; they were issued two stark white uniforms and two powder puff blue with assorted covers, a sweater, underwear, white shoes with rubber heels, and stockings, all of which fit into seabags. Then, they loaded onto a truck again and were dropped off at a female barracks. They went in, sorted it out, and showered. Gates showed up as they were about to turn in. "Ladies. We need a list of you and your specialties, and we can develop a roster."

They lined up and stated their names. Gates needed clarification about the spellings, so she handed it back to them to complete. She took the top copy of the roster, left a roll of masking tape and a grease marker, and told them to use it until the name tags were ready.

"You will all have at least eight hours of rest. Keep an eye on the clock. Shifts will be scheduled for 12-hour intervals but could easily drag on to 14-16. The emergency should last no more than three weeks. The uniforms are yours to keep, as we are eternally grateful for your help. Hey, I only have 24 names here. I was told there were 25 of you."

Kim-Yee spoke up. "That would be Gwen. She died during landing," she said, ending softly.

Gates nodded and asked, "Cause of death?"

"Broken neck." She tried not to cry.

Gates noticed her discomfort and motioned her out into the hall. "Time of death?"

"Around 9?" she said shakily.

Gates tucked her clipboard under her arm, grabbed her by the shoulders, and said, "Honey, you did well. You kept them together, focused, and alive. I've got nurses, but you are now considered combat nurses because you have been through the 'Fields of Fire,' and no one is a basket case. You are their leader, now officially."

She tucked her head into Gates' arms, who embraced her and said softly,

"Let it all out. There, there, you're fine." After several minutes, she held her at arm's length and handed her a kerchief.

"I'm sorry!" she said, almost weeping again.

"No. No. You're crying, not because you are weak. It's because you are human. You've just experienced a great amount of mental and physical trauma. But you must stay strong. Don't break down in front of the others."

"How can I do that?" she asked, hiccupping because of the tears. "I find a supply closet and cry my heart out when necessary. Now, are we good?" Gates said.

"Yes, ma'am," she said. Then she turned around, strode into the barracks, found her bed, and fell asleep instantly. She didn't dream at all. She just slept.

She awoke to the girls chattering away. They looked at the duty roster and a map of the base and saw where they were about the mess hall and the hospital. Everything was within a few blocks' radii. A Uniform Regulation Training manual was placed at the foot of each bed,

where she noticed a locker was. A paper clip was on the page called "How to wear the uniform smartly."

She read this out loud to them. "Members of the Navy Nurse Corps are required to possess all of the articles of the uniform prescribed except the raincoat as that will be issued on an as-needed basis…Any plain white uniform can be worn if it prescribes the regulation length of skirt and sleeves, white cuff links, the Navy Nurses Corps cap, plain white stockings, and plain white oxfords with rubber heels. Ward Uniform shall consist of 6 indoor white, three caps, and two pins on markings."

Agnes asked, "Well, they only gave us two of everything, so I guess we are okay, right?"

"Yeah, and if they say anything, ask them to provide what's missing. Now, where was I?" She continued, "Nurses shall always have a watch in good repair on their person. The white uniform shall consist of a skirt attached to the bodice at the waistline and a button-down front with white detachable buttons. The bodice shall be gathered into the waist at the front and back; the skirt shall be gathered into the waist at the back only. A loose belt shall be worn. This uniform shall have a convertible collar three ¼ inches wide at the back and shall be buttoned up to the throat if desired but shall normally be open at the throat. The skirt shall be of a length that conforms to the current length of wearing apparel. (See plate 76)."

Then, she went over to the billboard and checked the uniform of the day.

It said light duty. She consulted the manual and determined it was the blue one. However, some were grey. They all donned their uniforms and checked each other to ensure they presented smartly, and then they all walked to the mess hall and had breakfast. Afterward, they reported to their duty stations. The chaos from the day before had quieted down some, but there was still a sense of urgency. They got instructions from those they were relieving and went to task.

One day, Kim-Yee came around a corner with her hands full and passed by an admiral. He noticed her, and an aide walked up, asking her for her name and why she didn't salute. She told him, "I have my hands full and am on duty. I have lives to save. Get out of my way," and she went to push past him.

He blocked her and stated sharply, "I need your name, rank, and service number."

She huffed and said, "Chung, Kim-Yee, Nurse, no service number."

"Rank?" he said even more forcefully, "And why are you out of uniform?"

"NURSE!" she replied in kind.

"I can find out your service number," he said smugly.

"No, you can't because I don't have one," she said defiantly. "Belay that." Admiral Nimitz shot out, "Miss?"

"It's Mrs.," she said, her temper rising.

"Fine, Mrs. Chung. Where are you from?" he asked expectantly. "Hilo," she said in an exasperated tone.

"Hilo?" He said, thinking quickly, "We don't have any bases there." "No, Admiral, but there is a nursing school there, and Hilo is not an island. It's a city on the isle of Kona," she said crisply.

"And you are part of the cadets sent over?" he asked carefully.

This sent her over the edge; she placed the items she was carrying on a side table and strode towards him, stating forcefully, "We are not 'cadets,' we are fully qualified and board-certified Registered Nurses. We flew to your aid during the battle and lost one along the way. We've been working 16-hour days for the better part of a month. The wounded keep pouring in. This hospital was designed for 250 patients; we have over a thousand. We are tired, cranky, and want to go home."

He could see that she was close to tears, making him uncomfortable. "Then what's stopping you?" he asked, surprised.

"They are!" she gestured wildly at the rows of injured lining the hallway. "We were told we would only be here for the 'emergency,' but no relief has come."

"What time do you get off?" he asked.

"EXCUSE ME?" she snarled.

He realized how it came off and was stammering an apology, "No! Not like that. What time can you drop by my office so we can get to the bottom of this?"

"Oh…no, you don't!" she said, setting her face for battle. "We've been promised left and right that someone would take care of this. I'm not letting you out of my sight until then!" She hooked her arm in his and stated fiercely, "Wherever you go, I go until this is resolved!"

He called after the aide, "Have Mrs. Chung excused from her duties on my authorization." He turned and escorted her to the waiting car. "My office," he barked to the driver.

They went inside, and he asked her to sit down. Then he got on the phone. He then had several more brought in. Coffee was brought in, and he requested tea for her. She was so tired she passed out. When she awoke, he sat on the edge of a desk with a large legal pad and a different aide handing him documents.

\*\*\*\*\*\*

"He can tell the rest," Kim-Yee said as she calmly sipped her tea in the O-Club. She had a devil of a smile on. Miranda spoke to the children, and everyone understood, even though it was in Cantonese. They were tired, and she was taking them home. Daniel escorted them to the cab stand and paid the driver.

Then he returned to listen to the rest of the story.

# Admiral Nimitz

When he arrived at Pearl Harbor, everything was running in disaster mode. There were craters, bombed buildings, torn-up runways, twisted steel, and sunken ships everywhere. Then, he was touring the main hospital when he saw a nurse walking by who looked out of place. Her uniform needed to be corrected. He couldn't determine what, but her hair wasn't regulation, and her bearing was all wrong. When challenged, she whirled on them and told them what had happened.

"Okay, here's what I've gathered so far. When you landed, you were called Mercy Flight 7 with 25 guardians on board. You list one dead, and it was recorded. You all did emergency medicine triage on the runway at Hickam and were sent to the main hospital. Afterward, you were put under the command of Captain Gates. She got you all fed, clothed, and billeted. Then, she established a duty roster and was given orders to report to the Hospital ship Potemkin for duties in and around the Coral Sea. You then fell under the command of Colonel Means, who was also shipped out on the same hospital ship. We lost several nurses in the attack, and you just happened to fill in the gaps because you all kept to the duty roster without fail. No one knew you were civilians, and because of the crush of patients, military uniform standards went out the wayside. Hence where we are today."

"Then to whom do we report?" She asked.

"Well, to no one, but ultimately to me," he said.

"What are you going to do about it?" She wiped her eyes, pouring herself some more tea and filling his.

"Well, first things first. You all need to be paid, and we've been overworking you all, so I've authorized the paymaster to give you double the standard rate of military nurses. This is a one-time deal. Half can be sent back to your families immediately, and you may draw the other half in person. I also learned about a Cadet Nursing Program; my staff thought you were part of it. Yet another reason you all slipped through the cracks. But that's for untrained personnel. I want to hire all of you and put you into service as a Home Guard and Ready Reserve Nurses Corp. You will not leave the Hawaiian Islands. What do you think about that?" he asked.

"I think I'm the wrong person to be talking to about that," she said frankly.

"Well then, let's talk to your fellow Nurses about it," he said excitedly.

"No. We need to fly to Hilo and talk to Mother Superior about it," she said.

"Why?"

"Because they paid for our education, and we have responsibilities to the communities we trained for."

He felt sucker-punched, and he should have thought of it. "Okay, just let me get a couple of things straightened out, and then we will go." He lifted the phone, said, "Get me a flight to Hilo and amend that letter of intent with the following information…" and rattled it off. She gathered herself, and they walked out of the office, down the hallway, out the door, and down the steps to the waiting car. "Airfield.," he said.

They boarded the plane several minutes later, and she was seated across from him. The leather seat was luxurious, and the appointments were lavish. Coffee was served, and he pulled out a flask and poured some in. He offered her the flask, and she took it and gave it a healthy pull, then handed it back. He was impressed with this 5'1" ball of fury.

The flight was uneventful, with zero turbulence, and it was over before she could get used to it. They landed and disembarked. No car was waiting, not even a Jeep. A soldier called out from a guard hut. "Come in here to warm up, sir." It was windy and cold. But the shack was warm. It had a hot plate with a boiler of coffee on it. There was a tin for bread and a toaster.

"I'm afraid all I can offer you is some coffee and toast. They just woke up and are fueling a car for you. But the crisp air causes moisture, so they need to decant it properly. Otherwise, it could gum up."

"Coffee and toast sound great!" he said as he grabbed a cup and poured himself one. He offered her some, but she refused. The guard charged the toaster, and when it popped up into the air, he caught it expertly with the plate. He handed it to her with a smile, and she passed it to Nimitz. He noticed she was shivering, so he gave her a watch cloak. She took it gratefully and nodded thanks.

They heard a horn honking later and climbed into a three-seater Bantam Jeep. It had no cover. Nimitz moved the passenger seat, and Kim-Yee climbed into the back.

"What's the name of the place where we are going?"

"Sacred Heart Nursing School," she said.

The driver shrugged.

It's off the Queen Lille o Kalani Highway, the large white building that looks like a hospital?" she spoke.

"Oh, that one. Got it," and the driver peeled out.

They drove through the darkness and saw the early morning dawn, and as they pulled in and went into the courtyard, they noticed all the buildings were dark.

"Are they awake?" Nimitz asked.

"Yes. They have just finished prayers and should be coming out about now," she said as heavy wooden doors opened and lamplight spilled out, carving its amber glow through the darkness.

She jumped out and ran towards an older woman in a nun's habit.

"Mother Superior," she said excitedly as she embraced her.

"Are you back, child? Where are the others?" she asked, surveying the empty courtyard.

"Not quite," she said as she turned and motioned for Nimitz to join them.

"This is Admiral Nimitz," she said, introducing him.

"What happened to the other one?"

"I replaced him," he said.

"Come. We are just going to break bread. Get out of the cold. Join us." She turned towards the kitchen hearth.

He followed them and sat at the long wooden table. Finger bowls were set, and all stood. Heads were bowed, and the prayer of thanks was given. He saw fresh pineapple, a large chunk of bread with butter and honey, a boiled egg, and a Stein of beer. Good.

They ate, and he let them get caught up. He enjoyed the meal and the silence. They talked among themselves but in hushed, reverent tones. All the sisters had a sense of grace and calm reverence about them. He could tell that they were patient but also stern. He waited for recognition, kept quiet, and enjoyed the meal.

"I'm sorry, Admiral. We were just getting caught up. Tell me, have you found Gwen's body?"

"Gwen?" he asked.

"Yes, the nurse who died upon the crash landing. That one," she said flatly.

He pulled out a small notebook and jotted it down, stating, "I'll have to get back to you on that."

"When will I get my Nurses back?" she asked.

"That's a little more problematic..." he started.

"Really? Why?" She asked, raising one eyebrow.

"Because we still have over 4,000 wounded and are running out of places to put them," he said.

"Then send the convalescence cases to us. That should alleviate some of the pressure. There are several nursing homes around the islands as well. Some abandoned estates could be shifted to this measure, providing you send resources to help. We have Nursing Assistants and Nursing Students that could use the practice."

"That all sounds fine and good," he said, writing it down. "But I need to keep your nurses for the time being."

"I'm afraid that is just not possible. They have duties and obligations that have been unfulfilled for a month," she said, her tone getting slightly sharp.

"Mother Superior, I have a letter from the President of the United States of America that authorizes me to acquire all resources necessary for the war effort. This includes trained personnel. I would rather not use it. Instead, I offer a partnership. Now, normally, how many Registered Nurses can you crank out annually? 25?"

"That's correct."

"How about if we provide you with the resources to turn out over 150?" he asked excitedly.

"That's preposterous. We don't have the means," she began.

"We could provide it," he said as she rose and walked down the hall. She was swift, and he raced to catch up to her.

"I'm all ears," she said as they came to her office and sat down.

He was not used to being on this side of a desk, which would be a hard sell. "A Registered Nurse takes 36 months to train, right? We have developed a curriculum that brings it down to 30 months. There is also an LPN course that takes half the time. We might even be able to get it down to one year. And a Nursing Assistant cohort that takes six months; therefore, if we follow your logic and purchase or rent these abandoned estates and upfit them, then run separate revolving cohorts running day and night, we should be able to have candidates regularly."

"That won't work—the two shifts. Everything else sounds reasonable, and if we run on Saturdays and year-round, we might be able to accommodate. Plus, we have several cohorts running already. I would need to see the accelerated curriculum to plan to crash the current cohorts into compliance. However, that still doesn't explain how we house all these additional students. Then we would need more labs, classrooms, library space, and instructors."

"All could be constructed, rented, or up-fitted," he said.

"How about my nurses; what are your plans?" she asked.

"I want to hire them. But it's entirely voluntary. We would also pay you twice their training costs. I have a check for you to fill out regarding that," he said.

"And if they don't want to work for you?"

"Then their obligations stand, and I will send them back," he said.

"So, how will we solve the problem of the communities they were supposed to serve?"

"We will establish clinics in those communities and make it part of the training."

"Why would you want LPNs over RNs?" She asked.

His mind was racing to keep up when Kim-Yee, sensing he was out of his depth, cut in, "It takes half of the time, and the jobs are quite different. If you let the RNs manage the LPNs, you have a more elegant and effective care cycle. The LPNs can care for routine needs, and the RNs can run IVs and administer medication."

"And the Nursing Assistants, why are they necessary at all?" Mother Superior asked.

Kim-Yee answered, "Because they can take care of order filling of supplies, observation, meal service, general wound, and dressing care. Filling each category allows for the greater care of more patients. Thus alleviating the pressure and allowing the higher trained personnel more time for critical care needs."

He just smiled and nodded.

"Once trained, I don't want them to disappear into the military machine; what kind of safeguards are you offering?" Mother Superior asked.

94

"They will be sworn in as a Home Guard/Reserve Nursing Corps for the Territory. They will not leave the Hawaiian Islands. I have it in writing." he said.

"I wish to see both letters," she asked.

"Here you are," he said as he passed them over.

She took the first one, then turned around and placed it into the potbelly stove.

"I like this one better," she said as she rose. "Well then, let's be on our way."

"To where?" he asked.

"Why to Pearl." she said, "I need to see my girls." They went to the courtyard. She walked towards the Jeep and grabbed an apple crate, which she used to climb aboard, then reached down and retrieved it and set it down. He was impressed. Now he saw where Kim-Yee got her character from. They went back to the airfield and climbed aboard, then took off.

Once they landed, they were whisked away to the nurse's barracks in the car. She met with them and came out with three Nurses with packed musette bags after about an hour. "These three don't wish to remain. They are married and want to stay with their communities. I will draft you a check for the difference."

"Not necessary. Use the funds to hire an architect and at least three handymen. Their first project should be to build their housing. Then, acquire the buildings you need and enough supplies to get you started. Send your requirements to my office, and we will get work crews and supplies to you. You may take my car," he said as the driver came out to help load the bags.

"Now what?" Kim-Yee asked.

"Now we will get you all sworn in and into an officers training cadre," he said. "It shouldn't take more than 30 days."

She thanked him, saluted, and went to her barracks.

# Family Life

The story ended, and Nimitz motioned for another round and asked, "So, how did you meet?"

She said, "I had just finished OCS and was staying at the BOQ, and he checked in, and I noticed that he was wearing a grey uniform. I had not seen that before, and when he opened his window, I asked him to come out to the pool. He did, and that was that."

"It can't be that simple," Nimitz countered. Daniel replied, "It was. We met and hit it off."

"Why were you staying at the BOQ?" Nimitz asked.

She replied, "Because I was waiting for my sister and children to arrive, and the house wasn't ready yet."

"When did you find out she had two children?" he asked quizzically.

"Right after she told me her age and just before I proposed to her," he said, looking at her longingly.

She blushed.

Nimitz said, "Just from looking at you all at the table, I thought you had been married for quite some time."

She replied, "Nope. Just ten days."

"All of that in ten days?" he asked, perplexed.

"Yes, sir," he said. "It's getting late, and we have taken up enough of your time." He motioned for the check, and when the bill arrived, Nimitz grabbed it and signed it. He held up his hands to the couple and said, "No. No. This one is on me."

They thanked him, went to the taxi stand, and got a cab home. When they arrived, Miranda was frantically trying to scrub the kitchen, tears in her eyes. They rushed to her side and helped her up. Kim-Yee went to her nurse's valise, also known as the 'Battle Bag,' got a small flashlight, and told her to follow her finger in Chinese, left then right, then sent her off to bed. When she returned, she said, "She needs glasses."

"I think Hailey might as well. I saw her squinting, trying to read a book."

"What's your schedule for tomorrow?"

"I'm free," he replied.

"Good, then we'll fetch the wagon and go to the market," she said as she donned an apron and resumed cleaning. He rolled up his sleeves, and everything was squared away in a few minutes. The dried Chinese herbs and spices took the biggest hit and went into the bin. They shut off the lights, checked on the children, showered, and went to bed.

The next thing he knew, she was shaking him awake. He shot up in full combat mode. He looked around for the source of the alarm and saw it was still dark outside. "What?" he asked, exasperated.

She was already dressed. "Get up, sleepyhead. Time to go to the market," she said happily.

He rose and put on a casual shirt and some slacks, making a mental note to purchase casual clothes for working around the house. Then he put on a light jacket, grabbed a flashlight, and they crept out of the house. They walked the three blocks to the O-Club to retrieve the wagon. Then he started it up and asked her where they were going.

"Down to the wharf in Honolulu, silly; it's where the wet market is," she smirked.

"I didn't know that," he said, looking at the clock and seeing that it was only 3:30. "What's the rush?" he asked.

"We want to get there before all the good stuff is gone," she said.

They drove on the highway and saw the harbor was lit up. She motioned for him to park and then ran down the hill, dragging him along, giggling like a schoolgirl. They ran past what looked to be a farmers' market, but she was headed for the tanks of fish and seafood. She got to the shrimp monger, and he pulled some out of a bucket the size of his hand. They haggled for a bit in Chinese, and then both nodded. He weighed them out and rolled them in butcher paper. She pulled a rice sack from her purse, and he placed it inside. She handed him the bag, and they went to the next booth. This one had fish heads, and she wanted five. Three was too few, and four was out of the question.

He asked, "What's wrong with four?"

There was a sharp intake of breath from them both. "Ayah!" she said, "Four is the number for death, old Chinese superstition." She paid the man and then handed him the parcel. They went down three more stalls, and she picked out several redfish with the heads still on them. Then, some flounder and a sizable chunk of tuna. He felt like a pack mule.

Then, it was a left turn in the spice and herbs section. They were arranged in wooden bins, and you picked what you wanted; they measured it with a handheld scale with little weights on the side. They were placed in little wax paper packets. She put these directly into her purse. Then they returned to the front of the market, where she shopped for several vegetables. All of which were packed into a crate. Next, they went to buy rice. She picked out a 50-pound bag, and a young man picked it up and followed them to the car. He tipped him a quarter, and they drove back to the house and quietly loaded the groceries. All the seafood went into the icebox, and the vegetables were stored on the side where they would stay cool.

She got a piece of salted pork from the icebox and then added broken pieces of rice. Then added water and boiled it. Once it was simmering, she left it alone.

"What would you like for breakfast?" she asked.

"Pancakes."

"I don't know how to make that," she replied.

"I do. It's easy," he said, standing up and putting on the apron. "It's just flour, eggs, and milk."

She got the ingredients, and he put the right amounts together, grabbed an iron skillet, and warmed it up on the stove. He added some lard, waited for it to get hot enough, and then poured the batter. He asked her for some butter, and when the disks had enough bubbles on one side, he expertly flipped one over. Then, when they fluffed up just enough, he placed them on a plate. In no time, he had several stacks of pancakes. He buttered them up and put them up top in the warmer. Then he asked for bacon and cooked it up.

Kim-Yee got a kettle on and made hot tea. Then Miranda wandered into the kitchen in her bathrobe, all bleary-eyed, asking what was

Happening. They replied in unison, "Pancakes for breakfast."

Hailey smelled the aroma and came staggering into the kitchen. Her mother walked up to her and smelled her breath. She didn't say anything; she just pointed to the bathroom. Hailey rolled her eyes in disgust and stormed off to brush her teeth, acting like a martyr. While the ladies were setting the table, he checked on Jack, who was snoring away, oblivious to the comings and goings in the kitchen. He left the room and asked, "Where's the pancake syrup?"

"Uhm. We don't have any," Kim-Yee said, shrugging.

"No worries, I'll just have to improvise." He got to work. He grabbed powdered sugar and sifted it over the first stack he placed on the table. Then grabbed some strawberries and sliced them, then added some sugar to the small saucepan and melted it over them. He got a glaze working and poured it over the following stack. Miranda gave him some molasses, and he ran that over the last pile. Then he poured himself a cup of coffee and grabbed the milk, and they sat down for breakfast. It was 06:30.

Hailey liked the strawberry pancakes and ate a double helping of bacon. Jack wandered into the kitchen in his onesie, dragging along his blanket. He held his hands out to be picked up, and Daniel placed him in his highchair. A plate with a pancake covered with confectioners' sugar was placed in front of him, along with a small fork. His mom cut the pancake and went to feed it to him, and he shook his head and said, "No!" Then he proceeded to feed himself. He brightened at the taste and squealed with delight at the new flavor. He ate all of it and held out the plate for another. He was given the molasses this time, and he wrinkled his nose up at that one. So, Daniel traded him for the strawberry. He nodded and said, "Good!" then, "Dink?"

Daniel looked puzzled and then said, "Drink?"

Jack nodded, pointing at Hailey's glass of milk, "Dink!"

He nodded and filled a small bamboo cup with milk, which he passed to Jack. He looked at it and frowned. "No glass for you, young man... Not yet!" he said, smiling.

Jack agreed and lifted the cup to his lips, and slurped away. They all laughed as it dribbled down his chin. He stopped and then wiped the

Milk mustache off with the back of his hand, saying, "Ah!" looking real pleased with himself.

Then breakfast was over, and the washing up was done. The next thing to do was to go grocery shopping. Kim-Yee announced, "All right, troops, we need to get over to the commissary before it gets picked clean, so we must leave in 10 minutes." They scrambled and were all ready and loaded up into the car.

They drove over and went grocery shopping. He tried to load Jack in the cart, but he was squirming and kicking, so he put him down and saw that Jack wanted to help push the cart, so he obliged. They needed pancake syrup, margarine, eggs, flour, cornmeal, coffee, Cheerios, powdered milk for Jack, a chicken, bacon, bread, beans, ground meat, Kraft macaroni and cheese for the children, rice flour, a pork roast, Worcestershire sauce, red food coloring, potatoes, yellow onions, white pepper, green onions, shallots, eggplant, spinach, and salt.

Hailey saw a few girls from school, so she wandered over to them, and soon they were talking animatedly. She was telling them all about her trip to the O-Club. He smiled and continued down the aisle. When he got to the coffee, they were all out. He frowned and then saw Postum, a coffee substitute. He grimaced. He had that at basic during bivouac; it was nasty stuff. He would have to see if any was available off base since it was grown on Kona. He couldn't imagine that they couldn't buy coffee locally.

Then he turned to the baking goods aisle and saw that the bags of sugar had shrunk down to 2 pounds, which was the monthly allotment. This was new to him as he spent his time on ships, and his mother and sisters did the grocery shopping. He had grown up eating out of their garden, and his uncle Bob had a sugar cane plantation, so they had access to sugar, sorghum, and molasses.

When he got to the produce aisle, he grabbed a few eggplants, spinach, and tomatoes, plus cucumber, and his wife came from the butcher's counter with pork chops all wrapped up and asked, "Why are you buying spinach and Aubergines?"

"What's an Aubergine?" he asked.

She picked up the purple vegetable. "This is an Aubergine!"

"Oh? We call them eggplants," he said.

"Why?" she asked, puzzled.

"I don't know. Why do you call them that name?" he asked.

She laughed as she said, "I don't know either. But why are they in the cart?"

"Because I wanted to make some Greek food for y'all," he said mysteriously.

"What's it called?" she asked, now intrigued.

"Moussaka," he said.

"Spinach and <u>Aubergines</u> with tomatoes and cucumbers; how do you eat that?" she said quizzically.

"No, the moussaka and tomatoes go together. The spinach is for spanakopita. But we need some feta cheese."

"What kind of dish is the spinach-o-pita?" she said as she struggled with the name.

"It's a spinach pie, and we need leeks." They went in search of them and picked up some olive oil.

When they got home, he made a salad of tomatoes, onions, cucumbers, and feta; he added olive oil and some herbs and spices. He set them in the icebox and set about making moussaka. He sliced the eggplants lengthwise, drizzled them with olive oil, and roasted them for about 25 minutes. While that was cooking, he browned the ground meat and added salt and pepper. Then he greased up a pan and added a layer of eggplant, sliced tomatoes, and some grated parmigiana. He layered it up like lasagna, then added the last layer of cheese and baked it for 30 minutes. They had it for lunch, and everyone enjoyed it. Then Hailey asked if they could go to the beach, and they all got dressed and ran across the highway. She seemed a little miffed, and he asked her what was wrong.

She answered, "Why can't we go to Waikiki Beach, where all my friends are?"

"Why didn't you ask that in the first place?" They trundled back across the highway, into the wagon, and drove to Honolulu. Once they arrived, he could see why she wanted to be there. There were a lot of families, and she saw a few of her friends and ran over to them. He

She watched them and Jack, who happily played in the sand with a shovel and bucket. After a while, Hailey came over, saying she was thirsty. So, he opened the cooler and gave her a bottle of lemonade. He had also packed a couple of ham sandwiches, which disappeared quickly. Around 16:00, he told Kim-Yee that he wanted to get out of the sun, go to a Greek market, and pick up a few things. She wanted to come with him, and Miranda offered to stay behind with the children.

They drove to the ethnic quarter, and he went into a Hispanic bakery and got a bunch of pastries, then over to the Greek Market, where he picked up some baklava, Gyro flatbread, and some yogurt. Then they returned to the beach, picked up everyone, and went home. Then, off to the showers, and they had leftovers for dinner. The children were put to bed, and he and his wife sat on the veranda watching the stars and the moon.

They all slept late, dressed, and went to the O-Club for Sunday Brunch the next day. It was magnificent. They had a carving station for ham, lamb, and roast beef. There were omelets made to order, eggs Benedict, and sausages. The children were on their best behavior, getting many compliments for that. Jack liked the fresh pears and Jell-O.

Then, he drove them out to the pier to show them the types of boats that he had been driving the past few days. He also noticed that some Corvettes and Frigates were in the slips, and he knew that would be next on the agenda.

He then drove them up to the observatory on Lookout Mountain to enjoy the view. Then back to the house and a light dinner of spanakopita followed by baths and bed.

Then he was up and had breakfast of eggs and toast with bacon and coffee. He was reminding himself to get some more. He was out the door and driving to the Admin Center for class the next he knew. This week's plan was for Fleetwide Tactics and organizational interaction. The first half of the day was a lecture. The next half was in the War Room, acting out the battles from the past. Then, they were told to divide into teams for War Games. They only completed one round before time.

was called. Then, they assembled on the pier and ran the Frigates through the paces on Thursday. Friday was the Corvettes' turn, and Saturday was fleet-wide War Games in and around the bay. When he was done, it was 16:00, and he made it home for dinner. Then, on Sunday, he rested up by reading a Chess Magazine and playing a few games on his chessboard.

Hailey wandered in and looked out the window expectantly. After a few minutes, she gave up and asked him how to play. He could tell something was bothering her, so he asked.

"Nothing," she said dejectedly.

"Hailey, you keep staring out the window. What is it?" he asked a little sternly.

Tears welled up in her eyes. "He's not coming." "Who's not coming?" he asked, thinking it was a boy.

"My poppa. He said he was coming, but he was not there. Again!" She ran off to her room.

Daniel stood up and went to wake Jack from his nap. He then went to Hailey's room, where she had thrown herself on the bed. He said, "Get up and wash your face. We're going to get to the bottom of this." When Kim-Yee asked, he said he was taking them for a drive so she could have some quiet time. She agreed and went to lie down. He loaded them up into the wagon and drove out the gate.

"Where to?" he asked Hailey.

"Chung's Chop Suey House," she said quietly, shrinking slightly. He knew where it was just outside Honolulu on King Kamaya Maya Highway. When they pulled up, they could see the restaurant was closed for the day but could hear noises from the kitchen. So, he pulled to the side, went up to the screen door, and knocked. After about a minute, he heard a voice yell, "Go away. We closed for today."

He knocked harder.

The door was abruptly yanked open, and a small elderly Asian man of about 60 wearing glasses answered it in a dirty, bloody apron, holding a cleaver and cussing in Chinese.

"Aya! Can't you read?" Hailey called out, "Poppa?"

He stopped and saw her, laid down the cleaver, took the apron off, and opened the door. She ran to him, tears in her eyes. He embraced her and then looked up, asking, "Where is Jack?"

Daniel replied, "He's sleeping. I'll go get him." "Is Kim-Yee all right?" he asked, concerned.

"She's fine," he said. He was lifting the sleeping toddler and walking into the kitchen.

"Who you, military death notifier?" he asked, confused.

"No, sir. I'm her husband, Daniel," he said. "Your children were expecting you the week before last and this week. However, it bothers me that you didn't show up. Is there a reason?"

"Yeah. Stupid guards never let me in. I even showed them a court order for visitation, and they said to leave before I got shot. The base is on high alert for Japanese infiltrators. I say, 'Good thing I'm Chinese.' They are not amused! Point rifle and say, 'Go now!' I left; this week, a different set of guards but the same outcome," he said, exasperated.

"I'll check into that and see if I can't get you a pass. But here is our phone number," he said, passing a slip of paper to him.

"You hungry? I was finishing the cooking of char-suil." "I could eat, Mr. Chung.," said Daniel.

He replied, "Call me Garry. No use being so formal."

He went into the kitchen and whipped up a mountain of Chinese broccoli and stir-fried chicken within a few minutes. He put them into serving dishes onto a tray, and they walked to the anteroom. He served tea and ladled rice into bowls. They ate in relative silence, and Daniel thanked him for his hospitality.

"No worries." Garry said, "You good man. You make sure I see my kids. Can you leave for a few hours and get them later?"

"Sure," he said and left.

He drove around for a little while just enjoying the sunshine, parked the car, played a few chess games, and then returned to the Chop Suey House. When he arrived, the children were tired and ready to go home. Garry had packed a box with char-suil-bao, sliced pork, and ribs. Daniel tried to refuse it, but Garry was having none of that.

He drove the children home and saw his wife waiting for him.

On the veranda, he could tell she was vexed.

"Where did you go that took so long?" she asked menacingly.

"I took the children to see their father," he told her bluntly as he walked in and put the food on the table.

"You did WHAT?" she yelled, "Why would you do that? You had no right!"

"I have every right. I am their guardian as well. They are listed in the books as my heirs," he stated.

"What possessed you to do that?" she asked incredulously. "Because Hailey missed her father," he told her. "And it was wounding her spirit. I could not let it go on!"

She was in tears. "But you know what he did to me. How could you?"

"I simply went over to find out why he didn't show twice when she expected him," he said gently.

"And what story did he give you?" she asked sardonically.

"He tried to get on base twice and was told he could not. He even showed them the court order, but they told him to leave or be shot as a spy since he might be Japanese," he said.

Her eyes widened at the ramifications.

"He even told them, 'Well then, it is a good thing that I'm Chinese,' but that didn't work. I will see if I can get him a pass, but I'm not too hopeful," he said gravely.

She hugged him in an apology, saying, "You were only trying to do what was right. That's why I love you. That's why I married you because you are an honorable man. Next time, I'll take them."

"Well, you will need some driving lessons in the 'Beast'! And let's give Miranda some as well. She needs to get signed up for driving lessons."

"Let's go inside and have some of that roast pork," she said, smiling and licking her lips.

# XO

When he arrived at the lecture hall, he found a note to report to the pier. They divided into teams when he arrived and went to their respective ships. Two groups went to Patrol Craft and two to Cutters. They each got aboard and got them out into open water. Then, they were given targets to fire upon and a series of coordinated maneuvers.

"Hard to port," Daniel called out from the bridge of the Patrol Craft.

"Hard to port, aye," said the rating as he turned the wheel.

"Turn 355 degrees relative. Contact on. Pursue 20 knots. Range?"

"Turning 355 degrees relative. Pursue 20 knots."

The sonar called out, "11,000 yards."

"Fire five-inch guns as she bears."

Coleman, the Executive Officer, called out to the 5-inch guns, "Fire all batteries as she bears."

"Contact bearing at 30 degrees relative," called a relay man.

"Contact bearing 30 degrees relative. Noted. Keep firing." "Turn to 139 and fire all port side torpedoes."

"Turn to 139, aye!" called the helmsman.

The XO called out, "Firing port side torpedoes. All three fired electrically."

The ship made the turn to starboard to line up another shot. The XO called, "Portside torpedoes reloaded."

"Range to target one?" "9,000 yards," called sonar.

"Tell all batteries to ceasefire."

"All batteries cease-fire." "Time to impact?"

"Impact in five seconds," called a watchstander.

"We have red dye. Good hit. Second hit. They are done for," called the XO gleefully.

"How long until the second contact?"

"About three minutes. The range is one mile," answered Sonar.

"Fire remaining starboard torpedoes."

"Firing starboard torpedoes," the XO said, "Hang fire, hang fire!" They heard a loud bang and screams coming from amidships.

The fire alarm was rung, and the announcement was given, "All fire control parties report to amidship. All corpsmen prep to receive casualties."

Daniel grabbed a flare pistol from the holder at the side door, stepped out onto the rail, ensured a charge was loaded, and fired it into the air at a 45-degree elevation away from the ship. He called out, "Helm, come to a full stop. XO declare an emergency! Hangfire of torpedoes and casualties incoming. Sound the horn."

There was a very loud, "WHHOOOP, WHHOOOOP, WHHOOP," and a bell clanged, letting the rest of the flotilla know that an emergency was declared.

"XO, you have the bridge."

"XO has the bridge, aye. Coxswain Sherman, you have the bridge," he called out as he ran after the captain.

When Daniel arrived, he saw three ratings slumped on the deck whimpering. He had grabbed an emergency kit and opened it up, tearing open the cloth covers for the pressure bandages. He rolled one over and saw that his hand was mangled, and his skin was clammy and grey. His XO arrived a few seconds later with a blanket and used it to tamp out the smoldering of their clothing.

The corpsmen were the next to arrive, and they shoved their way to the wounded and had them rolled onto stretchers and carried away to the aid stations with ruthless efficiency. He stood dumbfounded and went to the head to wash the blood off his hands. Then, they both returned to the bridge, and he assumed command. They solemnly set course for a return to the pier. They tied up, and the wounded were carried off the gangplank to awaiting ambulances, who rolled out with their sirens blaring.

Major Garrison met them on board and asked for an after-action report. It took them about 20 minutes to write it. He then informed all crew involved to meet in the galley to determine the events that left three ratings maimed.

"Lt. Core, you are the commanding officer of this Patrol Craft 113?"

"Yes, sir, I am."

"Tell me in your own words what happened?"

"We were undergoing a routine training exercise, and all equipment had been inspected before launch. We had fired a brace of three torpedoes at contact one and got two hits. We then turned starboard to bearing 139 and attempted to fire the next set. When we got a hang fire from the controller, the explosion happened. After relieving the bridge to the EX-O, I was the first officer on the scene. I grabbed a medical kit containing morphine and rolled over a rating who had injuries to the left hand. His skin was ashen and grey, and he was going into shock. The EX-O arrived after transferring control of the ship to Coxswain Sherman. He brought a fire blanket and tamped out the smoldering clothing of the crew members. The corpsmen arrived and administered first aid, removing the casualties to medical."

The ratings were next to deliver testimony and were much the same. "I was on the port side reloading the torpedoes when I heard a buzz and a snap, then smelled cordite and felt the blast. Since I was behind the tubes, I was protected from the fireball."

"Anything else you wish to add?" "No, sir."

"Thank you. Please sign your statements, and you are free to go." The major turned and told Daniel and Coleman, "Follow me." They went to a briefing room, and he closed the door. "Why in God's name, did you both leave the bridge?"

"Because we needed to get to the men," the XO stated.

"Wrong! There are over 60 trained men aboard. Your job! Your mission is to lead. Not to try and play hero! What if those other torpedoes had cooked off and blown? Then the ship would be stuck with barely a Coxswain to pilot it while you were under attack."

"But sir, it was only a drill," said Coleman.

"True, but we train so we don't have to think. You failed the simulation, not because of the disaster but because you both made a fatal mistake. Now, we drill to learn from our mistakes. Sometimes

People are hurt in training, and sometimes they die. You have a team, so use them. Don't let this happen again!"

"Aye, aye, sir," they both said in unison and hung their heads at the rebuke.

"Dismissed. All shipboard drills will be suspended until further notice. Go home and take a day off. Clear your heads. Write up reports on this incident and what you learned. Also, write reports on every person you have interacted with in this class through training and workup. What are their strengths and weaknesses? How well they handled the exercises and where they need improvement."

He went home, had a quick dinner, and wrote the reports until 23:00. Then off to bed and back at it again. He kept thinking about how the failure happened but couldn't come up with anything.

On Saturday, he reported to the pier, and they spent two days going through the ships' emergency procedures, paying attention to the engine rooms and at-sea repairs. All of them performed all the functions of the enlisted men, from chowing down in the mess hall to swinging up to a cramped bunk in a crowded compartment. They learned how to pump shells and bullets from their weapons and roll depth charges from racks. Firing K and Y guns launch rocket bombs from hedgehogs and mousetraps. There were many drills, and not everyone made the grade. Those that washed out were given back to the Navy to be assigned elsewhere.

On Monday, when they returned to the pier, five were given orders to board a plane and fly to the mainland. He wasn't even allowed to call home and slept on the plane. When he arrived, he called home first and told her he was away for a few days and couldn't tell her more, but he'd be back soon.

After all the calls home were made, they all were driven to the bay to board their respective ships. His was a minesweeper, and they were to be underway in an hour. He was given the title of Executive Officer. His duty was to help escort the ship to Pearl in convoy. Once he arrived, he would be given more orders. But it looked like it would take about a week to do the crossing. So, he went to work. He met with the captain and was given a stack of files to review.

These were the jackets of his officers and those standing bridge watches.

Since this was a simple escort duty, he didn't need all the files for the whole crew. The ship was going through sea trials, and only a skeleton crew was on board. Also, most ratings were using this cruise as their final exam for striking. He was given five hours to get familiar with the crew and the boat. Then, he was expected to stand watch. He should eat no later than an hour before his watch. So, he went off to his cabin to review the personnel records. Most of them were recent graduates from various schools and Annapolis. There were also two middies on their first cruise. He had never dealt with midshipmen as they were always in Officer Country. But he knew he would get acquainted with them shortly, either in the Officer's Mess or on watch.

Daniel checked the time and decided to eat as the middle watch was coming up. He left his quarters and headed to the mess. He noticed ratings were moving around anxiously, so he stopped one and asked what was going on.

"Sonar thinks we are being shadowed by a submarine," the passing rating said.

"Why haven't we gone to action stations?" Daniel asked.

The rating shrugged and continued down the corridor. He picked up the nearest phone and called the bridge. The head of the watch told him that it was routine. They were under silent running. Continue duty as planned. This made him a little nervous, but he complied. Two others were assembled when he arrived at the mess: Midshipman Wright and Lt. Junior Grade Evans. Both stood as he entered, then sat as directed by him. A steward came in and placed the serving dishes on the linen-covered table. Each person had their setting that had the name of the ship emblazoned. There was coffee, lemonade, and water. Since Wright was the most junior, he served. Tonight's dinner was lamb curry with rice and potatoes. The vegetables were lintels, and the bread was flatbread. Grace was said after all the food was served; the meal began. He asked the middy about his time at Annapolis and how long he would be on loan.

"Just for the summer, sir," he responded anxiously. He then asked Evans which ships he had served on.

"This is my first, sir. I've just completed training; how about yourself?" Evans asked.

"This is my second ship in the Navy. I served on a destroyer for two years," he said.

"Did you get busted down?" asked Wright.

"No. Nothing like that. I served in the gunnery department as a rating for two years. I was recently promoted, and they needed this boat transferred to Pearl," he explained. They both visibly relaxed. But he could see their confusion, so he decided to tell them an abbreviated version of events.

"I was battlefield promoted, and as I had several years as a harbor pilot, they decided to accelerate my advancement. This is my first time as Executive Officer." They ate the meal in relative silence after that. Then, it was time to relieve the others. He entered the bridge and signed off his relief. The watches were changed, orders were given, and they continued for four hours. Every thirty minutes, the bells rang, and he had the lookouts report anything of interest. He also checked with radar and sonar teams, but no changes.

With his watch over, he went off duty for eight hours, went to his cabin, and retrieved his Dopp kit, skivvies, t-shirt, and shower shoes. He showered, shaved, and brushed his teeth, then turned in. He awoke to feel refreshed and went to chow. Lunch was corned beef with cabbage, potatoes, and crusty French bread; banana pudding was served for dessert. Then, off to the forenoon watch, much like the last watch. They saw dolphins running alongside and schools of tuna off the starboard side.

He was given word to report to the captain at the end of the watch. The captain asked about his watches, his subordinates' opinions, and any remarks of other watchstanders.

He responded, "All appear competent and easily fulfilled their assignments."

"How is the ship handling?" the captain asked.

"Fine, sir. Nothing to report so far."

"Good, then we will increase speed to 20 knots."

"Excellent, sir. By your leave?" Daniel said as he requested permission to be dismissed.

The shipboard watches were routine, and he made it back to Pearl without problems. He was told to disembark and report to Admin for further orders. He went by the office, but it was closed. So, he went home and showered, then crawled into bed.

His wife rolled over and kissed him, then went back to snoring. He passed out, and the next thing he knew, the children were crawling all over him, squealing, "Daddy's home!"

He smiled at the attention and asked, "What day is it?"

"It's Sunday, silly," said Kim-Yee, laughing as she wore her silk robe.

He got up, dressed in civilian clothing, and went to breakfast. He could see they had a new appliance, a crockpot, and the congee smelled terrific. Miranda had sliced fresh ginger and green onions, which he liberally sprinkled in the bowl, then added the rice porridge. He asked what the meat was, and Miranda replied, "Pig trotters."

He looked confused and got it, "Pig feet?" "Yes. That!"

she said, almost relieved.

Kim-Yee made sure that both children were at the table. Jack had his bowl of oatmeal with brown sugar, and Hailey had Cheerios. She got herself a cup of hot tea and a bowl of congee. Then she said, "So tell me about your adventure."

"Yeah, Dad. Where did you go? What did you do, and why so secret?" Hailey asked.

"Just a routine ferrying of a ship from San Francisco to here," he replied. "What kind of ship?" "A

minesweeper."

"Was it any fun?" Hailey asked eagerly.

"Well, we saw a few dolphins and some tuna. By the way, how was the tuna?" he asked.

Kim-Yee looked startled at the question and responded, "I haven't decided how to use it.

He then turned to Jack and asked him how his week was. He replied, "Good. Yummy. Love Poppa." He smiled and asked Hailey about her week.

"Fine. We got out of school, and there was a carnival on the last day," she said.

He asked Miranda about her week, and she said, "Good. Studying for a license. Had two lessons so far. Used sis' car."

"Now, remember you will need to learn to drive the wagon," he said.

"Yeah, sure, but I need confidence, then past test. Then get experience with a big bus," she said sheepishly.

He smiled as he didn't understand their reluctance with the vehicle, but he'd been piloting large craft for years. It must just be a woman thing. He enjoyed spending a relaxing day with the family.

Around dinner time, he said, "Hey honey, I know what to do with that tuna."

"And what would that be?"

"I'll sear it, and then we can slice it and have it over a salad. You prep the salad, and I'll get started," he said, grabbing an apron.

He washed his hands, took out the cast iron skillet, and then pulled out a small bottle that blended 50% olive and 50% vegetable oil. He poured some into the skillet and turned on the flame. He let it heat up for a minute and removed the tuna from the fridge. He grabbed a tin of breadcrumbs and took out a plate. He spread the breadcrumbs on the plate and rolled the tuna in it. He then seared it for about a minute on each side. He removed it, placed it on a chopping board, and waited a minute to cool. Then, he began slicing it with the cleaver at an angle. The exterior of the meat was crisp, and the interior was rare. He then placed several slices on top of the salads. He also minced some ginger and added soy sauce and sesame oil to make a dressing he scooped over the salads. They then sat at the table and tried it.

"This is good," said Kim-Yee. "I would never have thought to do that with the tuna."

After dinner, the dishes were washed, and the children were put to bed. They went out on the veranda and watched the stars together. Arm in arm, they looked up to the sky and enjoyed each other's company.

"Danny?" she said.

"Yes?"

"Come back to me," she said with profound sadness. "I will," he said as he kissed her.

The next day, he reported to Admin and was told to report to class. Then, there were more lectures, and he reported to the pier for maneuvers on Friday. This time, he boarded a Frigate and took it out to sea for target practice. They fired the guns at various targets and then launched high and low depth charges, high being to fire them off and low to roll them over the side.

Then, the day was over, and he returned for more integrated maneuvers the following day. He was given orders to report to the airfield; this time, he could call and inform his wife that he would return soon. When he landed, he reported to the pier and was given orders for Taskforce 7 to report to Patrol Craft 234. When he arrived, the entire ship's company was in Navy Whites. After being pipped aboard, he was handed a plaque, went to the podium on deck, and read out the commission and letter of assumption of command. His second time at command.

They got underway, and he couldn't believe he had gone from a rating to an officer in only five months. His mind was reeling. This was not just a ferrying mission or a shakedown cruise. This was a ship to call his own. This crew depended on him to make good and sound decisions. He had to do his best, and he met with his Executive Officer and familiarized himself with his crew members by reading all their files.

# PC-234

He awoke to the calmness of the sea and the gentle rocking motion aboard the ship. Moving towards his safe, he opened it and removed his orders. They stated to continue to Pearl, where he attended a graduation ceremony and a reception—orders to follow.

The crossing was uneventful as the last, and he settled into a shipboard routine. There were no significant issues to resolve; all departments reported ready, willing, and able. There were no substantial leaks or damage, and all appeared well and sound with the ship. They pulled into the dock assignment, and the day before, he had word sent to his wife to come to the parade grounds for the ceremony at the appointed time.

He met with his classmates and was surprised to find that most had been assigned to Frigates and Corvettes, a couple had even been assigned to PT boats, and those were going with him on his next assignment, whatever that was.

The ceremony was begun with Admiral Nimitz officiating, and the certificates were handed out. Then, off to the O-Club for an outside Luau, complete with fire dancers and hula girls. Nimitz announced that he was proud of them for coming along so well and accomplishing so much in so little time. They were to have fun, and he would see them all at noon for the final Captain's Briefing.

The party went well into the night, and they had fun. They took a cab back home, and he kissed the children, showered, and made passionate love to his wife. He awoke around 10 am, had a late breakfast, said goodbye to all, and left for the briefing.

Nimitz told them they were headed to Midway Island to attack the Japanese. He needed this strike force to hit them hard and fast with irresistible force, even if they were punching above their weight. This could be the decisive battle that they were looking for. He wanted to knock out as many of their carriers as possible and had the means. However, remember that while the Japanese had been at war for over a decade, they had only been at war for six months.

"Trust your training, your crews, and yourselves. Good luck and good hunting," he said goodbye to Daniel.

Then, they boarded their ships and headed out.

If you have enjoyed this novel, please go online and leave an honest review. Amazon.com: A Time To Shine (WW2 Patrol Craft Series): 9781958297018: Corzo, Donovan D.: Books

# Bibliography

How the 1930s London Treaty Changed Navies: Kept Them Smaller and Less Deadly - Bright Hub Engineering.

Uniforms of the U.S. Navy 1942-1943

Battle of the Aleutian Islands - HISTORY

Pacific Naval Surface Battles (navy.mil)

NMUSN_Pamphlet_What's_in_Your_Seabag_20200414_RS.pdf (navy.mil)

If you enjoyed reading this novel, please leave an honest review online. Amazon.com: A Time To Shine (WW2 Patrol Craft Series Book 1) eBook: Corzo, Donovan: Kindle Store

Free Preview of Book 2 "Shine On: Invasion USA"

# PC 234: Morning Watch
# Battle of the Aleutian Islands, June 3, 1942

"Helm, come about to bearing 191.", called Daniel as he felt the wind whipping around the bridge on Patrol Craft 234. The sea was calm, and the clouds were few, but he could see a mass of black storm clouds and feel the freezing wind biting into his skin as the atmospheric pressure began to drop. The Patrol Craft was about 173 feet long, 450-ton, diesel engine with a single 3-inch gun which was open to the elements on deck, depth charges, anti-submarine rocket launchers, a 40mm cannon, and three double-barreled autocannons. In essence, it resembled a smaller version of a destroyer. Its typical job consists of convoy escort and anti-submarine warfare.

"191 Aye, aye, Captain.", called the helmsman dressed in a Navy work uniform, a soft collard chambray shirt with bell-bottom dungaree material pants, a navy blue knit belt, and a white cover.

"What do you think, skipper?" asks Waisner, a husky Scot from Salkehatchie, SC, who was his Executive Officer. They were dressed in Khaki Uniforms and had previously served on the USS Aberdeen in the Coral Sea, where the ship was hit, and all officers perished. Before the last Officer died, he promoted Daniel to Warrant Officer with acting Captaincy and was told to "FIGHT THE SHIP!" Well, he did. He fought the fires, the enemy, the elements, and the sea. He got the crew to safety, then was whisked away to Pearl Harbor to return as a Lieutenant Junior Grade five months later with his ship, PC 234. When he was reunited with Waisner, he saw that he was promoted to Warrant Officer, and he proudly gave Daniel the letter from Nimitz that said, "Congratulations on your first Command. Please accept this Officer as your XO with my compliments."

"I think we caught them with their pants down." He said, looking through the captured Japanese Binoculars with a 5-mile range.

"Time for some payback?"

"Indeed! Let's wake them up! The Cyclops is launching ready fighters."

Waisner nodded to the Yeoman, who pipped it through the ship's PA system. "GENERAL QUARTERS! GENERAL QUARTERS! This is not a drill; repeat, this is not a drill. All hands report to your battle stations. Lock down all watertight compartments and secure all loose items." The Klaxons rang out with that "AWHHOZZAH!" sound. The men were timed, and they were both impressed. The crew was starting to come together as a team. It seemed such a shame that they might not live through this battle. But it was what they trained for. His gunnery crews had trained incessantly for this engagement.

They had used the aircraft to tow airborne targets, and his teams had such excellent fire discipline that they could destroy the targets before other ships in the Task Force had a chance to target them.

"Here they come!" said Waisner, and they all heard the distinct sound of the Zero's engine. It had a high-pitched whine and a deep rumble and roar as it flew overhead with the pinging of lead as they strafed the ship. But they shot back, and the devastating interlocking fields of fire they had established made short work of the Zeros and, inside a minute, had downed two enemy planes. Good. But that was not their goal. They were running interference and making themselves a juicy target for the enemy. The real battle was raging elsewhere around Midway Island. They had to stay in the fight as they were part of a convoy of Q ships equipped with electronic countermeasures and radios with recordings on wire spools that made them appear much more than they were. They even had sonar microphones called hydrophones that made pinging noises like a squadron of submarines, plus they had pulled two retired World War One Flattop Carriers into the scrum, the Cyclops and Jupiter. Training planes (wooden mock-ups) had been stationed on the deck to sell the appearance of being a Carrier Group. It looked like the enemy was taking the bait. But he needed them to commit fully. They were the "Ghost Navy." Now, to pull it off. The name was GRB-SCW 112, but the crew called this float the "Garbage Scow." as most ships were barely seaworthy.

There was sporadic contact, which was okay with him since the weather obscured their size and disposition. The area was where the two ocean tides mixed the icy water from the Bering Sea clashed into the warm water from the Pacific, which created hefty winds and helped obscure them from the enemy, but it also worked both ways. They were far enough out to sea from their target that they shouldn't encounter any Maru, those darn merchant vessels that were up-fitted to act like PT boats that generally carried a large-bore machine gun or two and several torpedoes. But they might not have to worry about that or be unlucky enough to be spotted by surface vessels. For if they got too close, they could see through the ruse.

He remembered that right after the final tactical briefing, and before they left Pearl, Nimitz waylaid him and twelve Captains and adjourned to another meeting room. When he handed over the packets, he looked like the cat that had swallowed the canary and had a devilish smirk. He looked up, his eyes wide.

"Well...what do you think?"

"Are you sure?"

"Yes."

"Any practical reason as to why?"

"Let's see. We know where they should be and where we want them to be. But that's not guaranteed. So, I want you all to assemble this little flotilla and get them to commit! I don't want a kerfuffle or even a brawl. I want you to appear to be larger than life and wounded. Give them such a target-rich environment that they can't help themselves."

"But sir. Some of these vessels are listed as unfit for combat and barely seaworthy.", said Captain Anderhouse.

"You can do repairs underway. Just put minimal crews on them and put these inside the transport ship. Then release them, and you will be like a magician pulling a rabbit from a hat. I know there are risks. But there are always risks. Plus, I've rolled two defunct flattops to your flotilla, complete with trainer planes on the deck. You will have at least twelve, if not eighteen, working airplanes. The Commodore will more than likely use them for surveillance. I want them to think that we are so desperate at using these and holding them together with spit and baling wire."

"But we are."

Nimitz shrugged

"That's devious! What's the casualty expectation?" asked Daniel.

"No more than 25%."

"I see. So, what's the rendezvous point?" asked Anderson.

"Dutch Harbor, Aleutian Islands"

He smelled salt air and was pulled back from his reverie. Unfortunately, he also smelled diesel—lots of it in the wind. "Waisner," he called out.

"Yes, skipper?"

"We've got company. Roll out the barrels!"

The order was given, and the Transport ship heaved to and started to open its hull once they were close to a complete stop. The PT boats and a few damaged craft swarmed out, taking their assigned places.

A lookout called "Kate's on approach!" Which was a **Nakajima B5N** carrier-based torpedo bomber from the Japanese Imperial Navy

"Looks like we got their attention."

"Roger that!"

"Tell the carriers to launch the remaining fighters!" He thought to himself. 'Carriers.' What a laugh. The Jupiter was an old, converted Navy Fleet Collier with two launch catapults off each side and barely enough tarmac to arrest them once they landed. She had been built in 1919 and decommissioned in 1933 due to a force drawdown. Then, she was recommissioned and sent out to fight. In May, she was shot up by nine aircraft and was considered unrepairable since she was outclassed and ordered to be sent to the breakers. Then there was her sister ship, Cyclops, much worse for wear. So, since she had over $300,000 worth of repairs, Nimitz decided that the least he could do was use her one last time in a desperate gamble to try and sucker punch the Japanese Imperial Navy. It was the ultimate "Up Yours!" maneuver. Now, they had the enemy right where they wanted them. But would it be enough? He was given a merry band of misfits. Most of his crew were good at their jobs but played fast and loose with the rules, but over twenty had either been drawn from the brig or were on their way there. They were given a choice. Fight this one desperate battle, and their records will be purged. If they died, they would receive full military honors, and their dependents would receive the service members' $10,000 life insurance payment. Not a bad deal, and if they were all killed, the Navy still won because it had gotten rid of most of its bad apples. Overall, 4500 men were staffing these craft, operating with less than skeleton crews. Typically, two thousand were on one aircraft carrier. After the second pass of planes, he received the order for even-numbered ships to light their burn barrels. These were red barrels with chopped-up tires and were ignited with aviation fuel. Which would create roiling smoke that would give away their position and make the enemy think the battle was going badly for them.

Looking through the glasses again, he could see tiny black dots on the horizon. "Let's get cracking," he yelled as all ships opened fire on the fast-approaching planes. The order of battle was for them to stage themselves into a pinwheel while each carrier was to be at opposing ends of an inner circle with Jupiter as the Flagship. At the top was the Light Cruiser; the bottom had the Transport ship and a hospital ship at the dead center. All other assorted ships would run in a concentric circle, keeping distance and overlapping fields of fire. Any stricken vessels would then rotate to the inward spiral for protection. The ring would continue to shrink as more and more ships were damaged. It worked on paper and in theory. It was just a circle of the wagon's defense instead of the prairie on the ocean. Now, to put this plan into action.

He thought all these moving parts reminded him of the distinct features of a symphony and watching the conductor. The PT boats were the string section, the Transport ship percussion; the destroyers were brass, the Carriers the wind section, the Hospital ship tin phony, and the Opera Tannhauser was in his mind playing the Flight of the Valkyries. It felt weird to be sitting here on the command deck as a Lieutenant Junior Grade when he was a gunner's mate, not five months prior. But that's war, and he knew that they were all expendable. He had hoped they could fight the enemy to a standstill at worst, but how much damage could they inflict? They had sixteen working planes and two bombers and were about to be inundated with fighters. He had ensured they had set up a good firing solution and had positive interlocking fields of fire. So far, they had only encountered air cover two by two. The first pair were scouts, and the bombers came in right behind, trying to take out the Carriers. Where was the rest of the group? Were these four just lost? In anticipation of the commotion that Nimitz had requested, they had overloaded every spare inch of the decks with anti-aircraft emplacements. The PT boats were sporting anti-tank rifles, and the four merchant vessels had five-inch guns. These were known as "Q" ships. He had quite an impressive amount of firepower, but would it be enough?

The Zeroes came in hard and fast, and the guns opened with a steady ACK! ACK! ACK! Sound. Then, the reports started pouring in from the flotilla. His command deck had several speakers set up to try and coordinate the mess. Everything was recorded on the wire spools for posterity and later review. Arthur Lake calling, "Large swarm of aircraft Zeroes, Oscars Val's, Judy's and Kates. Get ready!" Each enemy aircraft was assigned nicknames, with Zeroes being the fighter planes most servicemen went up against. The Oscar was a smaller, nimbler fighter with two 12.7 mm machine guns; they were constantly refined and even upgraded to a self-sealing fuel tank and armor to protect the pilot. They could also carry two 250-kilogram bombs. Kates was the Torpedo bomber, and Val was the single-pilot dive bomber. Judy's were two-man dive bombers.

"Hammerhead six engaging," called a pilot.

"On your wing six, breaking right and windmilling."

"Good approach, firing" (Loud machine gun noise)

"Got him six; he's breaking up."

"Splash one."

Hammerhead four is down. They got HARRY!" said a nervous voice over the comm

He called over the TBS, "Keep it professional, people; rely on your training. We need reports!"

"Rodger sir, wilco! Hammerhead two, he's coming in from the sun. Barrel roll left, and I'll line him up" (Guns firing)

"Hammerhead three, where are you? I can't shake this one. I---" Then there was static. He hung his head and ordered Waisner to "Stay on this and coordinate with the pilots."

"They won't last two more minutes," said Waisner, exasperated.

"All we can do is fight and win or fight and die!" He had to turn his attention to the calls from the ships.

"Mantas one through five starting runs on Maru and one destroyer," came the call from the PT boats. They could hear the machine guns firing with their steady BBBRRRRTTTT, and then the BOOM! BOOM! BOOM! of the anti-tank rifles. Then, there were several whooshing sounds as they launched torpedoes at their targets. A fireball erupted, and he could hear cheers. But he knew that this fight was about to get expensive. He looked through the glasses and saw that one of the PT boats was on fire, and the two destroyers, Arthur Lake and Jean Laffite, had bracketed the oncoming destroyer that was just out of support range from the convoy. The PT boats had softened it up, and their five-inch guns were pounding it to scrap. He heard a loud boom at the six-clock position and saw one of the "Q" ships take a hit. But they were firing like madmen at the wave of fighters, and he saw several splashes into the sea.

"Dorian is lost." called a voice."

"Who is this?" he asked over the TBS.

"Sorry, sir, Jean Lafitte here. The Dorian just went under."

"Was she hit?"

"Jean Lafitte here: No, sir, I don't think so. She just slid under the water."

He made a mental tally and realized that he was down by four percent of manpower and 12 percent of ships between that and the PT boat. They were barely five minutes into the engagement.

Waisner threw a coffee cup, which shattered as he yelled, "SON OF A BITCH!"

He called out, "BELAY THAT! What's going on?" he said, marching sternly over to Waisner, who just hung his head at the rebuke." Sorry, sir," he mumbled, "We just lost all the planes."

"Then go coordinate with the "Q" ships, and we just lost the Dorian": "How many made it out?" he asked, his face ashen.

"None, she just went under!" he said frankly, and he turned to announce, "Tighten up your screen, people. Close those gaps and get ready for the next wave."

His men fought bravely, and he watched the Potemkin make a daring run at the Light Cruiser with the PT boats harrowing it, making it jog left and right. Meanwhile, Arthur Lake came in from the lee side and launched her depth charges high and at the oblique, which caused them to detonate in an airburst and tear into their forward guns. The entire forecastle was rent open, and fire slowly engulfed the ship. He saw two other explosions rip into her at the rear, and she cracked in half, with the two pieces drifting apart and collapsing into the sea. He was now down by three ships as another PT boat succumbed to its wounds.

His order of battle was starting to look ragged,
 as there had been a bulge when those seven ships went after the cruiser. So, he called out, "All vessels report back to your positions on the line."

A yeoman said, "Sir, we've managed to down 25 planes, 5 Kates, and the rest Zeroes!"

"Put it up on the board," he said tiredly, reaching for a coffee cup and downing the bitter contents two hours cold. Someone had even put a cigarette in it; he spits it out and continues.

The battle raged on, and the attrition started. He couldn't get a read on how many he was fighting. Were they part of a larger task force spun off to deal with him? He wasn't sure.

Two aircraft made it through the screen and were targeting his ship.

"Helm, come about starboard 30 degrees", he ordered.

"Starboard 30 degrees. Aye!" They fired the anti-aircraft guns and then 40 mm when they got closer. This turned his ship hard left, putting it in a placement to attack the aircraft and eventually bracket it. One was shot to pieces and splashed into the sea, barely missing his ship. Then they heard a dive bomber scream in from above, but it was at a poor attack angle and became a two-way gunnery battle. The main problem was that the only way to win was to blow the aircraft to smithereens and dodge the wreckage. Otherwise, they would just get hit with shrapnel.

"PORT SIDE TORPEDO BOMBER!" called a watchstander excitedly.

He turned his attention and saw the plane coming in about 40 feet above the water, and he was under his guns.

"HELM HARD, LEEWARD!" he yells.

"HARD LEEWARD AYE!" the helmsman says as he frantically spins the wheel madly to the left.

"Come on, come on, come ON!" he says as the ship groans and turns to the left, leaning upwards at about a 15-degree pitch. It was enough to give the gunners the correct angle to hit the aircraft, and it exploded. They might have hit the gas tank or the torpedo. But they didn't have time to think about it as aircraft was coming in from every angle. He saw another plane go down, and its ruptured gas tank spews a lethal arc of combustible fuel all over the Jupiter. The Japs had enough planes through the screen and were targeting the carriers. He saw a dive bomber climb to 1500 feet and start its run when a 30mm gun mount from LSC-512 took it out. Unfortunately, the engine struck amidships, killing many men. But the support ship had effectively screened the carrier. He saw a 500-pound bomb hit 512 and slam into the rudder, and now they can't steer.

Suddenly, he heard a crackle of static on the plane's squawk box. "Blue Squadron Leader is coming in high to assist. Protect the carriers."

"Roger that," calls Wiesner, "How many in your group?"

"Just four left, sir. We've been taking a pounding. They've attacked Dutch Harbor. We were out on patrol and found this fracas. We will cover but need to land, rearm, and refuel. We can't raise the carriers."

"We will signal it over," said Daniel as he nodded to his signalmen, who ran up flags to signal the carrier. A signalman relayed the request, and landings were approved.

Five minutes later, two planes touched down on the decks of the Cyclops while the other two performed a combat air patrol to cover them. The Jupiter was fighting the fires on the top deck and couldn't do anything else.

"Torpedo in the water starboard side!" called a watchstander.

"Range?"

"Half a mile?"

"Sonar, get me a bearing."

"342"

"Roger that, Helm, come about to 342 smartly.

"342 smartly, AYE sir!"

"Combing it," said Wiesner, which meant they had turned to bring the ship to parallel the torpedo. This presented a much smaller target.

"Fire depth charges high and low on 275."

"Firing high and low, AYE!" called the weapons officer.

A few seconds later, loud explosions were in the water off the starboard side. He looked through the binoculars and saw no oil slick or debris.

He heard more airplanes approaching the flotilla and called out. "Waisner, tell those planes to take off now!"

"Roger, that skipper!"

A few seconds later, he could see them roaring off the flattop. "WE only got half a load, but it's better than none.", called Blue Squadron Leader.

The two planes flying the cap then landed as well. Hopefully, they could get outfitted with more ammo and fuel in the next three minutes. The worst thing that could happen is that they ended up on the deck when the carrier was hit.

Twenty more enemy planes entered the theater of operations and went to work harrying the defenders. His group was making short work of those pilots who were rookies. But that still left half, and those remaining were exceptionally good and started attack runs in earnest.

He called the Combat Information Center, the CIC, to ask how many they were facing. It was barely the size of a broom closet with a map on a table and a yeoman.

"Well, skipper, overall, we are looking at two aircraft carriers, assorted cruisers, a few destroyers, a dozen support ships, and maybe half a dozen submarines."

"Well, where are they?"

"Strung out over a five-mile path. The volcanic ash is playing merry hell with our equipment and likewise for them. The tides and currents push us all over the place and for them. We have updated maps and the sounding of the local area. They might not.

The remaining planes had refueled and were airborne again. They chased off the attackers and ran down any stragglers. But now they were out of ammunition as they only had enough time to get 45 seconds of ammo, about 500 rounds. So, they did their best and started runs with almost no ammo to completely dry. They harassed the enemy and forced them into turns, which ran them into the waiting guns. Two hours later, the engagement was over, and they were told to turn to and head for Dutch Harbor. Two planes were left, and they landed on the Cyclops. He coordinated with a support ship to try and rescue anyone left in the water, as they could freeze to death in about 12 minutes. None were saved.

Several hours later, they pulled into the harbor and surveyed the damage. They had taken a pounding. There were bomb craters everywhere, and the fuel dumps were on fire. He could see crews adding foam to douse it. They were glad the island had good anchorage and pulled into a mooring area. He called out the commands to park the ship and told them to lower the gig. He ordered the men to be fed and turned the boat over to a junior officer while he and Waisner went ashore to turn in their reports and see what orders would follow.

www.ingramcontent.com/pod-product-compliance
Lightning Source LLC
Chambersburg PA
CBHW022032170626
46808CB00003B/1154